"What did your father mean— why do we have his blessing?"

Lazhar took a deep breath. "My father believes that you're the woman I'm marrying."

"How did that happen? What made him think we're getting married? I'm the wedding planner, not the bride." Emily thrust her fingers through her hair. "You have to tell him the truth. Now."

"I can't."

"You have to! He's going to notice when you say 'I do' and the woman next to you isn't me!"

"Yes, he would," Lazhar said grimly, "if he lives long enough to attend the wedding. My father's greatest wish, perhaps his dying wish, is that I marry. I can't wait six months to find a bride. I need one now. He already loves you, Emily, and wants you as part of our family."

Lazhar paused, then looked into her stunned eyes. "Marry me."

Dear Reader,

It's October, the time of year when crisper temperatures and waning daylight turns our attention to more indoor pursuits—such as reading! And we at Silhouette Special Edition are happy to supply you with the material. We begin with *Marrying Molly,* the next in bestselling author Christine Rimmer's BRAVO FAMILY TIES series. A small-town mayor who swore she'd break the family tradition of becoming a mother *before* she becomes a wife finds herself nonetheless in the very same predicament. And the father-to-be? The very man who's out to get her job....

THE PARKS EMPIRE series continues with Lois Faye Dyer's *The Prince's Bride,* in which a wedding planner called on to plan the wedding of an exotic prince learns that *she's* the bride-to-be! Next, in *The Devil You Know,* Laurie Paige continues her popular SEVEN DEVILS miniseries with the story of a woman determined to turn her marriage of convenience into the real thing. Patricia Kay begins her miniseries THE HATHAWAYS OF MORGAN CREEK, the story of a Texas baking dynasty (that's right, *baking!*), with *Nanny in Hiding,* in which a young mother on the run from her abusive ex seeks shelter in the home of Bryce Hathaway—and finds so much more. In *Wrong Twin, Right Man* by Laurie Campbell, a man who feels he failed his late wife terribly gets another chance to make it up—to her twin sister. At least he *thinks* she's her twin.... And in Wendy Warren's *Making Babies,* a newly divorced woman whose ex-husband denied her the baby she always wanted, finds a willing candidate—in the guilt-ridden lawyer who represented the creep in his divorce!

Enjoy all six of these reads, and come back again next month to see what's up in Silhouette Special Edition.

Take care,

Gail Chasan
Senior Editor

Please address questions and book requests to:
Silhouette Reader Service
U.S.: 3010 Walden Ave., P.O. Box 1325, Buffalo, NY 14269
Canadian: P.O. Box 609, Fort Erie, Ont. L2A 5X3

The Prince's Bride

LOIS FAYE DYER

Silhouette

SPECIAL EDITION

Published by Silhouette Books

America's Publisher of Contemporary Romance

Special thanks and acknowledgment are given to
Lois Faye Dyer for her contribution to
THE PARKS EMPIRE series.

For my niece Carol and her husband, Simon,
May you have a long and fruitful life together.
Be careful, strive to be happy and remember
to always be kind to one another.

SILHOUETTE BOOKS

ISBN 0-373-24640-4

THE PRINCE'S BRIDE

Visit Silhouette Books at www.eHarlequin.com

Printed in U.S.A.

Books by Lois Faye Dyer

Silhouette Special Edition

Lonesome Cowboy #1038
He's Got His Daddy's Eyes #1129
The Cowboy Takes a Wife #1198
The Only Cowboy for Caitlin #1253
Cattleman's Courtship #1306
Cattleman's Bride-To-Be #1457
Practice Makes Pregnant #1569
Cattleman's Heart #1605
The Prince's Bride #1640

LOIS FAYE DYER

lives on Washington State's beautiful Puget Sound with her husband, their yellow Lab, Maggie Mae, and two eccentric cats. She loves to hear from readers and you can write to her c/o Paperbacks Plus, 1618 Bay Street, Port Orchard, WA 98366.

THE PARKS EMPIRE

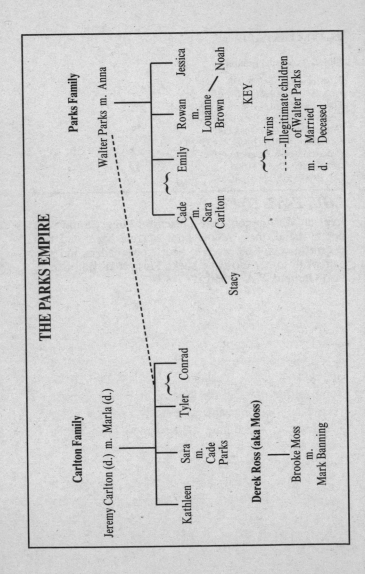

Carlton Family

Jeremy Carlton (d.) m. Marla (d.)

Kathleen

Sara
m.
Cade
Parks

Tyler — Conrad (twins)

Derek Ross (aka Moss)

Brooke Moss
m.
Mark Banning

Parks Family

Walter Parks m. Anna

Cade
m.
Sara
Carlton

Emily (twins)

Rowan
m.
Louanne
Brown

Jessica — Noah

Stacy

KEY

⎰ Twins
---- Illegitimate children of Walter Parks
m. Married
d. Deceased

Chapter One

"Brenda, do you think the newspaper stories about Father are true?" Emily Parks cradled a delicate teacup, warming her chilled fingers against the heated china. Despite the seventy-six-degree temperature outside, the kitchen of Walter Parks's San Francisco mansion was shady and cool. The windows in the dining alcove stood open and a slight breeze blew in off the Pacific, carrying the faint tang of salt and sea.

"Hard to say how much of the news reports a person can believe." The older woman's voice held doubt.

"I've always known Father was completely ruthless in business, but it's hard to believe that he'd be involved in anything criminal."

"Impossible to believe that he might do something illegal?" Brenda's eyes were shrewd behind her glasses. "Or difficult for you to accept that a member of your family might have done something outside the law."

Emily frowned, considering the question. "Maybe it's more that I simply don't want to believe that my father is capable of being involved in illegal business deals. Heaven knows he wasn't much of a father, but he's the only parent I've ever known." She glanced up at Brenda. Seated across the small walnut table, her plump, five-foot tall body encased in a soft blue uniform dress, the Parks's family housekeeper exuded concern and maternal affection. Brenda wasn't Emily's birth mother, but in all the ways that counted, she'd earned the right to be called "Mom." "If it wasn't for you, I would probably have grown up with a revolving group of nannies."

"*Hmmph.*" Brenda sniffed, her teacup clicking against the matching blue Wedgwood saucer as she lowered it with a snap. "Your father never had any sense when it came to hiring household help. How he managed to build that jewelry store of his into such a powerhouse is a constant puzzle to me."

Emily laughed. "That 'jewelry store' is San Francisco's version of New York's Tiffany's, Brenda. I'm sure Father has razor-sharp judgment when it comes to hiring employees for the business, but I've always thought the only intelligent thing he ever did for his personal life was to hire you to take care of us all those years ago."

Brenda's eyes twinkled. "Now that was a win-win situation. I was free to spoil you four children with no interference from your father. And in addition, he paid me a good salary." She patted her short gray hair and winked at Emily. "I was able to save enough to go traveling this year."

"How did you like Paris?" Emily loved hearing Brenda's tales of her travels. She longed to travel but for the moment, her growing business demanded every hour of her time.

"I loved it—the Champs Elysée, the Eiffel Tower, the Seine, the Monet paintings in the Louvre's Orangerie…" Her voice trailed off, a reminiscent smile curving her mouth. "I think I'd like to go back there for my honeymoon."

Emily's tea choked her in midswallow. She gasped and coughed, her eyes watering. It took a moment before she could speak coherently. "Honeymoon? What honeymoon? I didn't even know you were dating someone!"

"I'm not." Brenda said, her plump face serenely confident. "But I've answered a few personal ads and met some very nice men. I'm sure that I'll eventually find someone that matches my requirements for companionship.''

Emily couldn't hide her astonishment. "I didn't know you were interested in finding a husband, Brenda. I've always thought you were married to your job.''

"I was," Brenda agreed. "After my John passed away, you children were a blessing and caring for you filled every moment. I didn't have the time or the energy to lose myself in grief, thank goodness. But now that you're all out of the house and don't need me anymore, I've been thinking more and more about finding a male friend to spend the rest of my life with.''

"You're amazing." Emily slowly shook her head. "It takes a certain kind of courage to look for love even once, but searching twice in one's lifetime? You deserve a medal.''

"Courage?" Brenda looked at Emily over the rim of her glasses, a small frown creasing a line between her brows. "Why courage?''

"Because it seems to me that being loved once in a woman's life is a rare thing." Emily shrugged and lifted her cup. "The chances of it happening twice have got to be slim to none.''

"Oh, hon." Brenda's voice held sympathy and she covered Emily's free hand with her own atop the table. "Not all men are like your father and the men you've dated."

"Perhaps." She didn't bother to hide the skepticism she felt. She didn't need to—not with Brenda. "But if there are any nice guys in the world—with the exception of my brothers—I've never met them."

"So you've given up on finding a prince?"

"I'm afraid so."

Brenda sighed. She sipped her tea and a smile curved her mouth. "It's difficult to believe that the little girl who loved fairy tales has grown up to be a woman who doesn't believe in love. Remember how you declared that you were going to marry a prince when you grew up, just like Cinderella?"

"I remember." Emily's answering smile faded quickly. "That was a long time ago, Brenda. Unfortunately little girls grow up and have to live in the real world. Much as I would love to have a real family, with a husband who would love me and cherish our children—I've given up on finding my prince."

"I'm afraid your father has a lot to answer for." Brenda frowned, concern chasing away her smile. "He's ruined your faith in men. But all men aren't like Walter Parks. And someday, somewhere, the right man will come along and you'll have the family you've always wanted."

"I hope you're right, Brenda," Emily's voice

held a deep well of sadness. "It would be lovely to believe in fairy tales again."

"*Hmmph.*" Brenda shook her finger at her. "Just be sure you're paying attention so you can recognize him when he arrives. Not all princes ride a white horse and wear a crown, you know."

Emily laughed. "Yes, ma'am. I know. But while I'm waiting for him to ride up to my door, I think I'll spend my time building my company, since I suspect that dream has a much better chance of coming true."

Lazhar Eban was on his way to Walter Parks's library on the first floor of the sprawling mansion. Distracted by the contract he scanned while he walked, he turned left instead of right at the foot of the stairs, moved down a hallway and found himself standing just outside the kitchen, frozen by the conversation he'd accidentally overheard. The gold framed mirror hanging on the wall opposite him reflected the kitchen interior. On the far side of the room, tucked into a bay window looking out on the kitchen garden, was a comfortable dining nook where two women sat. The older woman was the housekeeper who'd shown him to his room late the night before. Lazhar instantly recognized the stunningly beautiful younger woman. Her thick mane of glossy hair was golden-brown, her eyes a bright green, and dimples flashed beside her lush mouth when she smiled. Emily Parks, Walter Parks's daughter, was the reason Lazhar had abruptly changed his busy schedule and flown to San Francisco.

Her photo had accompanied an addendum to a business proposal from her father, received at Lazhar's office only three days before.

Walter had approached him months earlier with a business proposal that had the potential to be lucrative for his country. He'd been on the verge of signing but had had second thoughts when the San Francisco newspapers publicly accused the American gem trader of questionable business practices. When he told Walter that he was reconsidering, Walter sweetened the deal by offering his daughter, Emily, as the bride Lazhar needed. The investigative report faxed to him from his security force as he flew over the Atlantic reflected an image of a sophisticated woman from a rich family, educated in private schools, who had built a thriving wedding consultant business in the years since graduation from college. His investigator could find no indication that Emily was currently involved with anyone, nor that she had been so since a canceled engagement some three years before. Emily appeared to be focused on her career, with her social life existing only as an extension of her work.

Given the fact that she was one of the most

beautiful women Lazhar had ever seen, he found it nearly impossible to believe that she wasn't involved with someone, but it appeared that she was not.

Which was all the better for him, he'd thought with satisfaction.

But in person, Emily Parks wasn't quite what he'd expected.

The beautiful face in the photo had fascinated him with the faint vulnerability behind the cool green gaze and the hint of passion in the sulky mouth. But the fleeting expression of stark loneliness that he glimpsed on Emily's face as she spoke with Brenda struck a powerful chord within him, calling to him on a level far deeper than her surface beauty.

She wanted to believe in fairy tales again.

A woman who once believed in fairy tales is a romantic, he thought, she'll never agree to a business merger marriage. His eyes narrowed as Emily pushed her hair back from her face and smiled warmly at Brenda. Even that small, graceful gesture from her was enough to send his blood pounding a little harder.

To hell with it. He wanted her. And he was going to have her, he vowed. It was good fortune that his need for a wife coincided with finding a woman that he wanted to bed.

But after overhearing Emily and Brenda's conversation, he knew he needed a change of plan. He was convinced there was no chance that she'd meekly agree to marry where her father commanded. Lazhar turned away from the mirror's reflection of the two women in the kitchen, moved silently back down the hallway, crossed the marble floor of the entry to the library and tapped on the heavy door.

"Come in."

Walter Parks looked up as Lazhar entered, a distracted frown quickly replaced by an affable smile of welcome.

"Lazhar, come in, come in." He gestured at the leather-covered chairs facing his desk. "Have a seat."

"Thank you." Lazhar dropped into the chair, his gaze flicking to the single sheet of paper in Walter's hand. "I hope I'm not interrupting?"

"No, not at all." Walter's fingers closed, slightly crumpling the sheet of paper before he dropped it atop his desk. "What can I do for you?"

"I've changed my mind about Emily."

Walter's tanned, lined face flushed, his cold brown eyes narrowing. "Why? Has she done something to offend you? Because if she has, I'll talk to her—"

Lazhar gestured abruptly, cutting off the older man's comments. "No, she's done nothing. In fact, I haven't even been introduced to her. I've simply rethought our original plan and decided that I don't want her to know about our business arrangement. I'll introduce myself and let matters take a more natural course.''

''Ah, I see.'' Beneath his salt and pepper hair, Walter's eyebrows rose, deepening the cynical expression on his leathered face. ''I take it that you're agreeing to my proposition, then?''

''If Emily agrees to become my bride, I'll sign the contract,'' Lazhar said. Walter's swift satisfaction was easy to read. ''But not until,'' Lazhar added.

Walter's mouth twisted in displeasure before the older man nodded his agreement.

''Excellent.'' Lazhar stood. ''I want your assurance that you won't mention anything about our arrangement to your daughter.''

''You have it.'' Walter rose and held out his hand.

The two shook hands, sealing the bargain.

''I'll be staying at the Fairmont Hotel on Nob Hill and driving there immediately. Since I don't want Emily to know about our plans, I think it's best that we aren't seen together before I have a chance to speak with her.''

''Very well.''

Lazhar strode out of the office, glancing back briefly. Walter was already focused on the sheet of paper he'd been studying when Lazhar first entered the room. He wondered briefly what had so riveted the businessman's attention but quickly forgot the incident as he crossed the entryway and moved swiftly up the stairs to one of the spacious guest rooms on the second floor.

"Your Highness?" A small man, hanging a snowy-white shirt in the closet, looked around with surprise.

"We're leaving, Pierre." Lazhar crossed the room to the desk and closed the lid on his laptop.

"Very well." The unflappable valet removed the shirt from its hanger and began to fold it.

Ten minutes later, his luggage tucked into the spacious trunk and Pierre sharing the front seat with the driver, Lazhar left the Parks estate and headed for downtown San Francisco and a luxurious Tower suite waiting for him at the historic Fairmont Hotel.

Meanwhile, Emily and Brenda were finishing their tea, unaware that they'd been observed by Walter's guest.

"I wonder if Father…" The back door burst open, startling Emily into silence. She didn't recognize the uniformed security guard who halted abruptly when he saw them.

"Sorry, ladies." His gaze swept the room. "We have an intruder on the grounds. Have you seen anyone?"

"No." Emily glanced at Brenda, who shook her head. "We haven't. Is this person dangerous?"

"I doubt it, ma'am. I think it's Maddy Jones, a reporter who's been trying to get past the gates to interview Mr. Parks."

"Oh, thank goodness, Andrew." Brenda's voice held heartfelt relief. "I was afraid a criminal was on the grounds. A reporter is a nuisance, to be sure, but only an annoyance."

"Yes, ma'am. We'll find her. If you see anything suspicious, let us know." The guard touched his hand to his hat and stepped back through the doorway.

"We will," Brenda called after him.

Emily pushed back her chair and stood. "I'd better get back to work, Brenda. Thanks so much for listening to me."

"You don't need to thank me." Brenda enveloped Emily in a quick hug. "I love having you visit. I don't see enough of you now that you don't live at home."

"I know. Work keeps me so busy." Emily linked arms with Brenda and they walked out the back door and around the house to the front courtyard, where her sporty little BMW was parked. "Why don't you meet me for lunch next week? There's a new French restaurant near my office that I'm sure you'll love."

"It's a date."

Emily hugged her goodbye and drove away, feeling immeasurably comforted by Brenda's down-to-earth wisdom and unfailing affection. As always, the older woman was a stable rock of sanity in what was often a dark world surrounding her father.

While Emily was leaving, Walter was frowning at the sheet of paper he'd picked up from his desktop the moment Prince Lazhar left his office. The letter was written by his daughter, Jessica, and addressed to his estranged wife, Anna, at the Switzerland sanitarium where she'd lived for many years. Cryptic though the words were, Jessica clearly stated that her mother's suffering would soon end and that Anna would be "out of her father's clutches" very soon.

"What the hell does she mean by that?" Walter muttered to himself, glaring at the sheet. He'd read the letter over and over, but couldn't decipher precisely what Jessica could be referring to. One thing he did know, he thought grimly, was that he had enough problems without his daughter and wife stirring up more. He wanted Anna to remain in Switzerland, safely tucked away as she had been during all the years since he'd first forced her to go there.

With quick decision, he picked up the phone and punched in the phone number for Sam Fields, an investigator he'd used in the past. He'd have Jessica followed and her movements reported to him. It was the easiest way to learn what she and her mother were up to.

Emily's office was organized chaos.

"It's barely nine o'clock and I'm already behind."

Emily glanced up. Her assistant, Jane, stood in the doorway, the neon-blue pencil tucked above her ear a bright spot of color against the corkscrew blond curls that brushed her shoulders. The bright blue was repeated in the paisley scarf draped artistically over one shoulder of her simple little black dress.

"It's crazy-busy today," Emily agreed. "Did you find the lilies for the Everston wedding?"

"Yes." Jane's pixie face lit with satisfaction. "It took five calls but I finally located some in Seattle. They're being flown down this afternoon."

"Excellent." Emily sighed with relief and took a sip of her vanilla latte. "How Mrs. Everston could have forgotten to tell us until the day before the wedding that her daughter simply must have lilies at the altar is beyond me."

Jane shrugged philosophically. "That's a mother-of-the-bride for you—stressed and forgetful. I'm just thankful she didn't want something that had to be flown in from South America or China!"

"Good point." Emily saluted Jane with her logo-stamped paper cup from the espresso stand on the corner. "It could have been worse."

"Emily?" Natalie, the receptionist in Emily's three-person office, joined Jane in the doorway. Her air of suppressed excitement was palpable.

Emily eyed her with curiosity. "What is it, Natalie?"

"You'll never guess who's on the phone."

"Who?" Emily and Jane waited expectantly.

"An aide to Prince Lazhar, the Crown Prince of Daniz."

Emily's eyes widened and she exchanged a quick, surprised glance with Jane. "Prince Lazhar? Of Daniz? What does he want?"

"He wants to schedule an appointment for the prince to meet with you this afternoon."

Emily didn't need to glance at her calendar. She already knew what her day looked like. She shook her head. "I can't possibly, Natalie. Maybe tomorrow." She flipped her desk calendar open to the following day.

"Emily, you can't tell a European prince that he has to go on a waiting list," Jane said firmly. "Especially not this prince. It's all over the tabloids that he's looking for a wife. Maybe he wants you to handle the wedding."

Emily was unconvinced. "I doubt it, Jane. You're talking about a royal wedding. I've never handled anything of that magnitude...I'm sure he'll hire a bigger firm, maybe from London or Paris, perhaps New York.''

"You'll never know unless you talk to him," Jane urged.

Emily glanced at Natalie and received an eager nod of agreement.

"All right." She turned the page of her calendar to today's date and skimmed it quickly. "This is impossible," she murmured, as she ran her fingertip down the list, shaking her head. "I really don't have any openings, but...tell his aide that I'll squeeze the prince in between the Benedict fitting and the Powell catering conference."

"Excellent." Natalie grinned. "I've always wanted to meet a real prince." She disappeared down the hall.

"You're squeezing a royal prince in between an Atlanta socialite and a California movie star?" Jane lifted her eyebrows.

"That's the best I could do. Katherine Powell is always late so I'm hoping I'll have a few moments before she makes her entrance. Speaking of which." Emily glanced at her watch. "I'm already behind."

"This is where I came in. Back to work for me." Jane waggled her fingers at Emily and disappeared down the hall. A moment later, Emily heard the murmur of her voice as she spoke on the phone.

"The prince of Daniz." Emily said softly, staring blankly at the blinking cursor on her computer screen. The news of the king of Daniz's declining health and his wish to see his son wed had been well chronicled in the press. What reason other than business could possibly have sparked his request for an appointment? Was it possible that the prince might actually be considering hiring her to plan his wedding? The prospect of the assignment and what it would do for the future of Creative Weddings was tantalizing.

She shook her head and yanked her thoughts back to the file open on her desk. She had far too much work to do today. Daydreaming about planning a royal wedding would have to wait.

Fortunately for Emily, the Atlanta socialite had booked a late luncheon and needed to cut her appointment with Emily short. Emily ushered the young bride-to-be and her mother out the door, walked to the ladies' room to freshen her makeup, and was just slicking color onto her lips when Natalie burst into the room.

"He's here!" Natalie's eyes sparkled with excitement. "And he's just as gorgeous in person as he is in print!"

"Is that possible?" Emily teased.

"Trust me." Natalie fanned her face with her

fingers. "In his case, it's more than possible. It's a fact."

"Now I'm even more curious about the mysterious prince," Emily commented. She gave her reflection in the mirror one last inspecting glance, smoothed her palm over the scarlet suit jacket and across the hip of her pencil-slim skirt, and satisfied that she was tidy, followed Natalie into the hallway. They reached the reception area and Natalie veered off to her desk near the entry, gesturing significantly across the room. A tall, dark-haired man stood with his back to them, looking at a collection of French Impressionist prints on the wall.

"Your Highness?"

He glanced over his shoulder as Emily approached, then turned to face her.

Oh my goodness, she thought as she met the impact of eyes so dark a brown that they appeared black. *Natalie was right, he's drop-dead gorgeous.*

His lashes narrowed, his gaze sweeping her from head to toe and leaving a trail of heat in its wake.

"Miss Parks?"

"Yes, I'm Emily Parks. And you must be Prince Lazhar." *And you,* she thought, *are a dangerous man.* Not only was he handsome, with hair as black and glossy as a crow's wing, olive skin stretched taut over the planes of high cheekbones, black lashes so long and thick that it seemed a crime to waste them on a man, and a powerful body that was six feet four inches of toned muscle and hard angles, but he fairly oozed testosterone and radiated sex appeal. She wasn't sure what protocol required when greeting a royal prince, but held out her hand and managed a polite smile.

"Please, call me Lazhar." He smiled and took her hand in his. His fingers and palm were slightly rough against her own smooth skin.

"Very well...Lazhar." Realizing that her hand was still enclosed in his warm, much larger one, she took a step back, the small, evasive movement slipping her hand from his. She gestured to the archway leading to the hall and the offices that opened off it. "Won't you come into my office?" She glanced at Natalie and found her pretending to read a file while slanting sideways, fascinated looks at the prince. "Natalie, will you bring us coffee, please."

"Right away."

Emily's skin prickled with awareness as Lazhar walking behind her out of the reception area and down the short hallway to her office. Something about him had set all of Emily's female instincts shrieking a warning. This was no tame, civilized male. Lazhar Eban threatened her feminine independence on a very basic level. It took all her composure to keep from canceling their appointment and finding an excuse to ask him to leave. Relieved that she could put some distance between them, she gestured to the two damask-covered armchairs arranged before her desk.

"Won't you have a seat." She rounded her desk and dropped into her chair, upholstered in a soft blue that echoed the damask of the armchairs, and folded her hands together atop the desk. "What can I do for you, Your Highness?"

Emily had handpicked the chairs facing her desk specifically because they were large enough to accommodate husbands-to-be and small enough not to overwhelm the more slender forms of their brides. But Lazhar made the chair he sat in seem small and his muscled, broad-shouldered body, combined with the sheer force of his presence, seemed to dominate the room.

"I'm getting married," he said, his gaze fastened on hers. "And I want you to organize the wedding."

Emily was speechless. She'd wondered whether this might be the reason for his appointment, but his statement still staggered her. She gathered her composure and nodded. "Very well." She flipped open her notebook and picked up her gold pen. "I'll need some parameters. What date have you scheduled for the wedding?" Pen poised, she looked at him, waiting.

"As soon as possible."

"You and your fiancée haven't picked a date?"

"No. Is that a problem?"

Carefully Emily placed her pen on the gleaming cherrywood desktop. "Perhaps not a 'problem,' exactly, but certainly a concern since it's impossible to begin planning without a time frame in mind. And I'm afraid our calendar is booked several months, sometimes more than a year, in advance."

"What's the earliest date that you're available?"

Emily wondered briefly if he was thinking of a small, private wedding. Surely a royal affair would be scheduled by the palace and the date set in stone? "Before I look at dates, perhaps we should discuss what sort of a wedding you wish to have. Depending on the preparations needed, we may be able to schedule your event sooner, rather than later."

Lazhar shrugged. "I'm afraid I don't have a lot of latitude in the wedding ceremony. Royal weddings in Daniz are ruled by tradition and our customs require that the celebration is a week-long affair."

Emily blinked, startled. "So," she said slowly, "you're asking me to plan a week-long celebration, including a royal ceremony, within as little time as possible?"

"The palace has event coordinators that will assist you. What I need is someone to plan, organize and delegate. And I'm willing to pay whatever is necessary to have you devote your time exclusively to the event in order to speed the process.''

Emily was stunned. A royal wedding on her résumé would open doors in Europe and the Middle East and had the potential to gain worldwide recognition for Creative Weddings. But it would mean working with the prince, and she wasn't sure that was wise. On the other hand, in her experience the groom rarely spent a great deal of time with the wedding consultant. The husbands-to-be were always more than happy to leave the details to their prospective brides. ''I assume that the wedding will be held in Daniz?''

''Yes.''

She toyed with her pen, stalling for time while she tried to absorb what he was saying. She glanced up at him through her lashes and found his dark gaze fastened on her, a slight air of tension surrounding him. ''May I ask why you chose my firm?''

''You were highly recommended by the Radissons,'' he said smoothly. ''Their daughter Angela is a good friend of my sister, who was a member of the wedding party.''

''Ah, of course.'' Emily instantly made the connection. Angela Radisson was a San Francisco society deb, several years younger than Emily, and wonderfully unspoiled. The wedding party had included several of Angela's college friends, one of whom had been a beautiful dark-haired young woman named Jenna. Gazing at Lazhar, sprawled casually across from her, she immediately saw the family resemblance. "I wasn't aware that Jenna Eban was a princess."

The grin that curved his mouth was wickedly charming. "My sister likes to shed the 'princess' title on occasion and pretend she's not royal. I'm not surprised that she didn't tell you, but I'm a little surprised that you didn't suspect."

"Why is that?" Emily absorbed the impact of the effect the smile had on his already handsome face.

"Because Jenna tends to be a magnet for the tabloids. It's good to know that they didn't spoil her fun."

"Ah. I see." Emily forced her attention back to the wedding. "Well." She picked up her pen and flipped the pages on her calendar, swiftly scanning appointments and calculating. "Depending on the expertise of your palace staff—and I assume they're accustomed to planning grand functions—?" She glanced up. Lazhar's nod of agreement reassured her. "Good. Then it may be possible to have the ceremony in six months." She frowned, shaking her head slightly. "But that's a very tight timetable. And I'll need to do an on-site inspection…" she murmured. Once again, she consulted her calendar before glancing up at Lazhar. "I'm afraid I'm fully booked for the next two weeks but I can carve out a four-day-weekend after that to fly to Daniz and meet with your people."

"That won't work."

Emily blinked. "What won't work?"

"I don't want to wait two weeks. I want you to start immediately. Preferably, this afternoon."

"I'm afraid that's impossible," she said coolly. "I have prior commitments that I can't reschedule."

For a moment he was silent, his enigmatic gaze meeting hers with an oddly assessing light. "So it's a question of your workload and timing, not of your willingness to begin the wedding preparations immediately?"

"Yes."

Emily's agreement seemed to satisfy him, for he nodded abruptly. "Very well. Then we're agreed that you will come to Daniz as soon as your calendar is cleared?"

"I believe that's mutually agreeable. I won't be able to give you a projected cost for our services until I've been to Daniz, however."

"That won't be a problem." He shot back the cuff of his shirt, frowned at his watch and stood. "I'm afraid I don't have time to discuss further details as I have another appointment this afternoon. Perhaps we can resolve the issue over dinner tonight.''

''Oh, but I—'' Emily broke off. Despite her instinct to distance herself from him, she couldn't afford to miss this opportunity. It's just business, she reminded herself. ''Very well, dinner would be good. Where would you like to meet?''

''I'll pick you up at seven.''

''I can meet you at the restaurant—I wouldn't want to inconvenience you.''

''It's not a problem.'' He smiled at her, a slow, wicked grin that curled her toes and shortened her ability to draw a breath. ''I look forward to it.''

He turned and left the room. Emily wilted in her chair and stared at the doorway where his elegantly clad, broad-shouldered body had just disappeared.

''Well?'' Natalie and Jane interrupted her, their faces alive with curiosity. ''What did he say?''

''He wants us to handle the arrangements for his wedding.''

They shrieked; Natalie did a quick dance while Jane clapped her hands with delight.

''This is excellent, Emily. What a coup! When do we start?''

''Not for at least two weeks—that's the earliest I can fly to Daniz.''

''What date is the wedding?'' Jane asked.

''There isn't a date, not yet. The prince wants it

scheduled as soon as possible but I told him I doubted it could be done in less than six months.''

''Six months? That's all?'' Jane's eyes rounded behind her wire-frame glasses. ''For a royal wedding? You're joking, right?''

''No. He insisted that he wants the ceremony scheduled as soon as possible and that the palace staff will assist.''

Jane looked doubtful. Natalie fairly bounced with excitement.

''I want to apply for a promotion to Jane's assistant—even if it only lasts through the wedding. I'll never have another chance to attend a royal wedding.''

Emily smiled at the younger woman's enthusiasm. ''If we really do plan this wedding, Natalie, I promise you can go with us.''

Natalie beamed with delight.

''So,'' Jane said, ''who's the lucky woman? Who is he marrying? She'll be a princess, and someday, the queen, right?''

''I don't know who he's marrying.'' Emily suddenly realized that Lazhar hadn't offered the information and she'd failed to ask. It wasn't like her to miss such a vital piece of data. ''I'm having dinner with him tonight...I'll ask him the name of his fiancée, among other things.''

''You're having dinner with him?'' Natalie's eyes widened.

"It's strictly business, Natalie," Emily said firmly. "He had an appointment and had to cut our discussion short so I…"

"Hello? Hello, is anyone here?"

The rich, throaty tones floated into the office.

"Yikes." Natalie hurried for the doorway. "That must be Katherine Powell!"

Jane and Emily exchanged a wry glance.

"She does love celebrities, doesn't she?" Jane said.

"Yes, she does," Emily chuckled with affection. "I think that's ninety percent of the reason that she works here."

"I can't wait to hear all the details—call me after you talk to the prince tonight, okay?"

"I will," Emily promised, then stood as Natalie ushered a stunningly beautiful woman into the room. "Good afternoon, Katherine."

Lazhar didn't have another appointment. But he wanted Emily to join him that evening and finishing their discussion seemed the easiest way to convince her. After meeting her, he was even more determined to marry her. He needed a wife; she wanted a husband and children. They'd both get what they wanted.

After talking with Emily in person, however, he was even more sure that she wouldn't marry him to further her father's business plans. Emily Parks was beautiful, with golden-brown hair, bright green eyes, smooth tanned skin that his fingers itched to touch, and dimples that flashed when she smiled. The fitted scarlet suit and high heels made the most of her slim figure and long legs and conveyed the image of an upwardly mobile businesswoman. But Lazhar saw a well-concealed vulnerability and wariness beneath her smooth, sophisticated exterior. If he hadn't overheard her conversation with the housekeeper at the Parks's estate, he might have missed it and accepted the surface image. But the yearning in her voice when she spoke with the housekeeper about a family and children made it impossible for him to see only her sleek, lovely exterior.

After meeting Emily, he was convinced she was the woman he wanted for his bride. Now, all he had to do was convince Emily.

Chapter Two

This is just a business dinner, Emily told herself that evening as she turned in front of the mirror to check the back of her dress. *There's no reason for me to be nervous.* The simple cocktail dress was a Vera Wang design, the off-the-shoulder black silk tasteful and perfect for a business dinner with royalty. Not that she'd ever had dinner with a prince before, she thought, refusing to consider that the butterflies fluttering in her midsection might be caused by Lazhar's handsome face and charming smile and not by his royal status.

She smoothed a hand over her hair, noting absentmindedly that it brushed against her shoulders; she made a mental note to call her hairdresser and schedule an appointment to have the thick fall trimmed a quarter of an inch. One last inspecting glance assured her that she was as ready as she'd ever be. She turned away from the mirror, picked up a tiny black handbag and left the bedroom.

The doorbell rang just as she entered the living room and she glanced at the antique French clock on the mantelpiece.

Seven o'clock. Not only is he royal, he's also punctual.

She pulled open the door and although she'd thought she was prepared to see him, still her breath hitched and she found herself staring helplessly at the man outside her entry. He took her breath away. In the hours since she'd seen him at the office, she'd managed to convince herself that he couldn't have been as heart-stoppingly handsome as she'd first thought. But she'd lied to herself, she realized as she met his gaze. He really was as sinfully sexy as she'd remembered.

"Good evening."

His gaze swept her from the crown of her head to her toes, making the return journey just as swiftly, his mouth curving in a smile. "Good evening. Ready to go?"

"Yes." Emily stepped across the threshold and pulled the door closed behind her.

He moved back, falling into step beside her as she walked toward the elevators.

"Do you like living here?" he asked, his tone curious as he surveyed the hallway while they waited for the lift.

"Yes, very much." Emily's gaze followed his, moving over the red and cream floral carpet, the pale green walls with their gold-framed prints, and the matching discreet name and numbers beside the six doors that opened off the short hallway. "I love living in the center of the city and though the building is older, it's well-maintained and secure."

"Ah. And security is important in San Francisco," he commented as the elevator pinged and the doors opened.

"I suppose it's important everywhere, don't you think?"

"Yes." His voice turned grim. "Very important."

He took her arm and ushered her into the lift, his body briefly brushing hers as he leaned past her to push the button for the lobby floor. The faint scent of soap and aftershave reached her, the slightly rough texture of his suit jacket teasing the bare skin of her arm. Although he was impeccably polite and made no overt moves, she felt crowded by him and too aware of his much bigger body. He was so blatantly male that he made her feel overwhelmingly feminine. She couldn't recall any other man of her acquaintance eliciting such a strong response.

"Does Daniz have a crime problem?" Emily asked, determined to conceal her reaction. She vividly remembered the photos she'd seen in a travel brochure of the small kingdom on the Mediterranean Sea. Tucked between the eastern border of Spain on one side and France's southern edge on the other, Daniz's sun-drenched beaches were adored by tourists and its fabled Jewel Market was equally revered by the gem industry. Crime didn't seem a part of that fairy tale picture.

"I suspect every country in the world has a problem with crime, some more so than others." Lazhar's deep voice sent a slow shiver up Emily's spine. "Daniz's crime rate has never been high when compared to many countries but there's always room for improvement. We've increased the police force and taken an aggressive proactive approach over the last few years and the result has been a decrease in all types of crime."

"Is this part of your plan for national security?" He raised an eyebrow in inquiry and Emily smiled. "I confess I did some online research this afternoon in an effort to learn a bit more about your country before we talked this evening. Part of what I learned is that you were appointed to lead the Daniz National Security Forces five years ago."

"Ah." His mouth quirked. "I hope you only

visited the official Daniz Web site and not the sites featuring gossip from the tabloids.''

Emily laughed. "I did visit the Daniz government site, but I also read a few very interesting tidbits at a site called Secrets of the Royal Families of Europe.''

Lazhar groaned and shook his head. ''I'm afraid to ask what you learned there. I hope you didn't believe anything you read.''

"Most of it sounded like pure fiction. Unless—'' she looked at him with interest ''—you really did fly across the Mediterranean on a hangglider to spend the night with a harem dancer?'' The swift expression of horror that flitted across his face made her laugh. "No?''

"Absolutely not.'' His deep voice held disgust.

"Pity.'' Emily sighed, watching him through the screen of her lashes. "I thought perhaps she was your fiancée.''

"No, definitely not.''

The elevator reached the lobby, the doors opening with silent efficiency. Two muscular men in dark suits stood sentry at the door to the street; they snapped to attention, one of them speaking into a small two-way radio as Lazhar took Emily's arm and they exited the elevator. They crossed the black and white marble floor and one of the guards opened the door while the other fell discreetly into step behind them. Outside, another black-clad, burly man held the door of a long black limousine open wide. Emily was about to enter the limo when someone called her name.

She paused and glanced down the street. "Hello." A smile lit her face. Her brother Cade was striding toward them along the sidewalk. "What are you doing here?"

"I'm picking up Stacy—she's visiting Anabeth."

"Oh, I wish I'd known she was near, I would have stopped in for a hug." Emily adored Cade's five-year-old daughter; the precocious little girl shared Emily's love of shopping and they'd formed a mutual admiration society of two. Stacy's friend Anabeth lived in the next apartment building and the two often shared playdates.

"I'll call you the next time I bring her over, I promise." Cade nodded at Lazhar and held out his hand. "Lazhar, it's good to see you. I didn't know you were in town."

"I've just arrived—the trip wasn't on my schedule and my aides didn't have time to contact you."

Emily glanced from her brother to Lazhar. "You two know each other?"

"Yes. Of course." Cade grinned at her. "But I didn't know you and Lazhar were acquainted."

"We just met today," she said calmly. Cade was her fraternal twin and loved to tease her as if they were still twelve-year-olds. When his eyes twinkled, she knew he'd jumped to the conclusion that she was dating the handsome prince and was going to comment. "But I'm looking forward to doing business with him," she said smoothly, before he could speak.

Cade blinked at her and she could almost see his brain shift gears.

"Business? What kind of business?"

"Wedding planning, of course," she said, leaning forward to press a kiss on his cheek. "Give my love to Stacy and tell her I'll see her tomorrow."

"Sure." Cade nodded at Lazhar as the prince handed Emily into the limousine. He bent to peer into the interior, his hazel gaze intent. "You're in good hands with Lazhar, Emily."

Emily barely had time to wonder what he meant by the cryptic comment before the bodyguard closed the door and the limo pulled smoothly away from the curb. She glanced back to see Cade standing on the sidewalk, watching them drive away.

"How is it that you know my brother?" she asked Lazhar as the car eased into traffic.

"We met some months ago when he came to Daniz to visit the Jewel Market."

"Ah," Emily replied. Cade was an attorney and he handled much of their father's contracts for the Parks jewelry store; he was being trained as the heir apparent to succeed when Walter retired. Not that anyone who knew Walter thought he would ever retire, in fact, it was generally agreed that he'd probably die at his desk, working on a new deal. But nevertheless, Walter considered Cade his heir and demanded that his son spend a large amount of time on Parks Empire business interests. "So you're in the gem industry, like my father?"

"Not quite like your father, I suspect," he corrected gently. "For centuries, the Daniz Jewel Market has been a center for international jewel dealers and gem trading is important to my country. Because my family rules Daniz, I'm involved by necessity with the Market, but gems aren't my sole business."

"So you're not obsessed with jewels?"

His dark eyes were grave. "No, Emily, I'm not obsessed with jewels. I have neither the time nor the inclination. I'm deeply committed to the people of Daniz and to my family and I find they require all my attention." He shrugged. "I suppose some might call the depth of that commitment obsessive, but I choose to believe otherwise."

"I find it admirable that you choose people over business interests," Emily commented, unable to look away from his warm gaze. "In my experience, such a choice is very unusual. My father's primary commitment is to his business…he's driven by the next negotiation and making each new contract bigger than the last, with more money, more perfect gems, higher profile clients. The men in his circle that I've met, no matter how old or young, all seem to feel the same. It's refreshing to meet someone who's involved in the gem industry but whose life is apparently not owned by it.''

Lazhar laughed, white teeth flashing against tanned skin, his dark eyes amused. ''I confess that I've met traders at the Jewel Market who were willing to sell their soul for the price of a rare diamond, ruby, or sapphire. But I'm not one of them.''

''I'd love to visit the Jewel Market,'' Emily said. ''I've heard it's a fascinating place.''

''I think so,'' Lazhar agreed. ''We've preserved the building and the interior much as it was when it was first built, three hundred years ago, by the King of Daniz and the Prince of Persia. The mosaic tiles on the floors and walls, the handmade carpets and wall hangings, the gold minarets...all are well worth seeing.'' He smiled at Emily. ''I'll give you a tour when you visit my country.''

''I'd like that very much.'' He really is charming, Emily thought. The limousine slowed and she realized that she'd been engrossed in their conversation and hadn't noticed their route. She glanced out the window and then back at the prince, puzzled. ''This looks like the airport.''

''It is.'' He agreed.

"We're having dinner at the airport?" She wasn't aware of a five-star restaurant located at the San Francisco International Airport. Certainly not a restaurant that a man of Lazhar's caliber would choose, she thought.

"Not at the airport."

The car slowed and parked beside a sleek jet. The bodyguard seated next to the driver leapt out and opened the door for Lazhar. He exited, turning to hold out a hand to Emily, and she followed him out onto the tarmac. The evening was warm and balmy; a slight breeze lifted her hair, skeining it across her face. She brushed it back, tucking it behind her ear.

They were standing a few feet from the steps leading up to the main cabin of a private jet. The logo on the tail spelled out Daniz in vivid blue and gold. Beside her, Lazhar spoke to one of the bodyguards in what Emily thought was French. Finished, the man nodded, bowed and reentered the car, which pulled away.

"This is your plane?" Curious, she glanced from the jet to Lazhar.

"Yes." He tucked her hand through the crook of his arm and led her toward the steps. "I think you'll find it comfortable."

Emily abruptly stopped walking, her movement halting Lazhar as well. "I'm sure I would," she said carefully. "If I were traveling on it, but I'm not."

"Actually we are." Lazhar's smile flashed, his dark eyes teasing. "And our destination is a surprise. I think you'll find the food well worth the trip."

"We're flying out of town for dinner?"

"Yes."

Uncertain, Emily hesitated. She didn't know Lazhar well enough to get aboard a plane with him headed for an unknown destination. On the other hand, Cade *did* know him well and had assured her that he was trustworthy. Her brother's recommendation overcame her innate wariness and she gave in.

"Very well—if you promise the food is worth the flight."

"I promise." Lazhar led her up the steps to the cabin.

"Good evening, Your Highness." The white-coated steward greeted them with a bow.

"Good evening, Carlos." Lazhar seated Emily in one of the high-backed, upholstered seats next to the window with a small table between them. Both chairs and table were bolted securely to the floor and the chairs had seat belts. Behind him, the steward closed the outer door as the powerful jet engines rumbled to life, vibrating the cabin floor beneath Emily's feet.

"I need to talk to the captain for a moment, please make yourself comfortable, I won't be long."

Emily murmured an assent, her gaze following Lazhar until he disappeared through the door at the end of the cabin. The summerweight, pale gray suit he wore was beautifully made and clearly custom tailored to fit his long legs and broad shoulders.

She sighed and shook her head at her own foolishness. Lazhar Eban was engaged to be married—already taken and off-limits. And even if he were available, he wasn't her type of man at all. He was much too high profile, too powerful and too rich—all qualities that her father also possessed. Emily had intimate knowledge of just how difficult it could be to live with such a man.

On the other hand, Lazhar Eban was quite possibly the handsomest, sexiest man she'd ever met.

"If you'll fasten your seat belt, ma'am, we're about to take off." The steward advised.

"Of course."

He nodded his thanks when Emily clipped the latch and tugged the belt snugly across her abdomen. He left the cabin, Emily assumed to take his own seat elsewhere, and in moments, the sleek jet taxied down a runway and lifted smoothly into the air. She glanced out the window to see the Golden Gate Bridge appear off the wingtip before fluffy white clouds obscured her view.

Lazhar must have had to remain in the cockpit with a seat belt on, until we're airborne, she thought as she gazed curiously around the luxurious cabin. The interior of the Daniz royal family's jet was unlike any private plane she'd ever been on. There wasn't a utilitarian piece of furniture in sight, even the sturdy chair she sat in was upholstered in a glorious deep blue fabric that felt like rough silk. Her feet rested on a thick carpet with jewel tones of scarlet-red, cobalt-blue, antique-gold and pearl-white that complemented the cabin fittings. The walls were a discreet, smooth pearly-white, the wooden doors a deep mahogany set into arched doorjambs that reminded her of Spanish architecture. A collection of small French Impressionist paintings were clustered on one wall, their muted colors glowing against gold frames. Emily's gaze lingered on the unique furnishings that made the plane's interior as comfortable as a lavish hotel suite, and she was reminded that Daniz bordered Spain, France and the Mediterranean. Clearly the royal family enjoyed the best of all their cultures.

The plane climbed steeply and it wasn't until it finally leveled out that Lazhar rejoined her, the steward following closely on his heels with a tray holding a chilled bottle of wine and two stemmed glasses.

Lazhar took the two filled glasses from Carlos's

tray and handed one to Emily. "To your health—and to our successful business enterprise."

"To a beautifully organized wedding ceremony," Emily responded, tilting her glass in salute before tasting the wine. "Mmm, delicious."

"It's a Spanish vintage from the Penedes region." Lazhar dropped into the chair next to her and lifted his glass to eye the golden liquid. "And a favorite of my father's."

"And of yours?"

"And of mine," he agreed.

"Would you like to have it served at your wedding?" Emily set the exquisitely cut wineglass on the parquet table that separated her chair from Lazhar's and took a small notebook and gold pen from her bag.

Lazhar shrugged. "Yes, of course. If you think it's appropriate."

"I think it's an excellent choice. I'll make a note to request that the caterer use it. What is it called?" He told her, his deep voice smoothly switching to Spanish. She wrote down the name, vintage and year, then closed her notebook and placed it on the table, her pen next to it, before picking up her wineglass once more. She took a sip and observed him over the rim of her glass. "Are you going to tell me where we're going for dinner and if the menu will be Spanish to match the wine? Or must I wait until we get there."

"We're having dinner aboard the plane."

"Aboard the plane?" Confused, Emily stared at him.

"But tomorrow," he continued, "we'll have lunch in Daniz. I'll have the palace chef uncork another favorite vintage for you to taste."

"I beg your pardon?" Emily was certain she'd misunderstood him. Daniz was at least a ten-hour flight away from San Francisco.

"By lunchtime tomorrow, we'll be in Daniz."

Emily was speechless. His gaze didn't flinch from hers, he seemed to be waiting for her to react to his blunt statement. Her surprise quickly gave way to anger and she returned her wineglass to the table with a snap.

"Are you telling me that this plane is flying to Daniz?"

"Yes."

"With me on it?"

"Yes."

"Without your asking me if I were willing to go to Daniz?"

"You told me this afternoon that you're willing to go to Daniz. It was only a question of the timing."

"I also told you that it would take at least two weeks to clear my calendar."

"Which is why I discussed the situation with your assistant, Jane, and why the staff from my embassy in San Francisco will be reporting to your office tomorrow. They'll do whatever your assistant requires of them until you return. They'll also install the necessary equipment to link your office to the palace media room so you can be in touch with your staff at any hour of the day or night, whenever you feel it necessary.''

Emily was furious. ''How kind of you. But that doesn't change the fact that you failed to ask for my permission to do any of those things. Nor did you bother telling me about your plans when you lured me aboard this plane.''

''I can only apologize. When I spoke with Jane she assured me that she would be happy to take your appointments over the next couple of weeks. She also told me that the chance to combine a holiday in Daniz with work was something that she firmly believed would be good for you.'' Lazhar paused, eyeing her. ''She seemed quite taken with the idea, in fact, she volunteered to go to your apartment to pack your bag and get your passport this evening.''

''Jane helped you with this conspiracy?''

''She assisted with the arrangements, yes.''

Emily fumed, silently wondering what on earth Jane could have been thinking.

''I know you might not like my method of getting you to come to Daniz, Emily, but I'm sincere about the limited time frame. I don't know how familiar you are with Daniz politics, but the news reports about my father's health are true. He's not well. We don't know how much time he has left and he wants to see me married as soon as possible. I want your firm to handle the wedding plans but I can't wait two weeks—not because I'm being difficult and high-handed, but because I don't know how long my father will be with us. And I'll do whatever is necessary to give him what he wants," he added grimly.

His words defused Emily's anger as little else could. She didn't have a good relationship with her own father, but she could understand a son's wish to please a dying father. "Very well," she said. "When you put it that way, there's little I can say. However," she added when she saw relief ease the tense lines of his face, "I want to talk to Jane about the office arrangements before I agree."

"I thought you might." He lifted the tabletop between them, revealing a telephone in the cabinet beneath. "While you're talking with her, I'll check with the pilot about our flight time."

Her temper still simmering, Emily pointedly waited until the door closed behind him before lifting the receiver and dialing, tapping her nails impatiently against the arm of her chair while she waited for Jane to pick up.

"Hello?"

"I'm going to fire you for this, Jane."

"Hi, Emily." Jane's voice held a smile, despite Emily's grim tones.

"I can't believe you did this—what were you thinking?"

"I was thinking that a) You've got a genuine shot at planning a royal wedding that would send Creative Wedding's status through the roof; b) You're so conscientious that you would never want the Benedicts or Katherine Powell, or any of your other clients, to feel that you gave royal wedding arrangements priority over theirs; and c) You can't miss this opportunity. It's just too good."

"I know all of this, Jane. I took it into consideration when I told Prince Lazhar that I could fly to Daniz in two weeks, after I cleared my calendar."

"But the prince made it very clear that he can't wait two weeks," Jane said. "And although I know you want to be there for each and every detail for your clients, Emily, I looked at your schedule for the next two weeks and I really can handle your appointments till you come home."

"What about your own work?"

"Most of what I've booked as priority for the next few weeks is glorified errand-running and double-checking details for the Andersen and Heaton weddings next month."

"Hmm." Emily sighed, still not totally convinced.

"Emily," Jane's voice coaxed. "We've known each other since high school. Have I ever lied to you?"

"No."

"Then trust me, going to Daniz is the best opportunity you've ever had to build your business. It's like found money. This could make Creative Weddings the most important bridal consultant firm in the U.S. Not to mention," Jane added persuasively. "That you're going to spend a week or more in one of the most beautiful countries on the Mediterranean. And you'll be staying in the palace. You haven't had a vacation since we left high school—this is the perfect chance."

"You're sure you won't be buried under at the office?"

"Positive. Besides, your prince said he's sending over staff from the Daniz Embassy. They're accustomed to dealing with diplomatic receptions and galas and they can do all the errand-running on my calendar while I'm free to deal with your appointments."

"All right," Emily said reluctantly. "You've convinced me. But I'm still not happy with the fact that neither you nor the prince asked me if I was willing."

"Hon, you would have refused," Jane said with an affectionate chuckle. "I can hardly get you to go out to dinner on a weekend because you're working. Getting you to agree to anything that takes you away from the office is difficult. You really need this break.''

Emily sighed. ''Brenda told me last week that she was worried that I was working too many hours.''

''Brenda's right,'' Jane said promptly.

''I'll expect you to stay in touch, daily,'' Emily said.

''Absolutely,'' Jane replied.

They discussed a few items on the morning's schedule before they rang off, after Jane promised to check in with Emily each day while she was in Daniz.

The receiver had barely settled onto the phone base when the cockpit door opened and Lazhar strode into the room.

Emily waited until he sat down next to her before she spoke, answering the unvoiced question in his eyes. ''Jane will handle my schedule while I'm in Daniz but she'll be in contact every day, and if something comes up that needs my attention, I'll fly home immediately.''

Relief mingled with satisfaction on his face and he nodded. ''This jet is at your disposal, should an emergency arise. And if all goes well, I'll fly you home when you've had time to tour my country, visit the palace, meet the people of Daniz and feel you have enough information to plan the wedding.''

Emily picked up her notepad and pen. ''I suppose that's reasonable,'' she said reluctantly. ''How long do you think that will take?''

''A week, perhaps two. It depends on when you feel you've seen enough to feel comfortable planning a wedding that fits within our culture.''

''I'll pencil in a week.'' Emily gave him a cool look. She'd always secretly longed for travel and adventure but her single-minded focus on building her company had taken up all her time. Of necessity, she'd put that dream on the back burner. Lazhar was unwittingly fulfilling one of her childhood wishes but she was still annoyed at his high-handed method of gaining her cooperation.

''A week,'' he repeated with a nod. Emily read satisfaction in his eyes before his gaze left hers. He pushed one of the buttons located in a key pad on the chair's armrest, then picked up the wine and refilled their glasses. As he was returning the bottle to the tabletop, the cabin door opened and the steward entered.

''Ah, Carlos,'' Lazhar greeted the man. ''We're ready for dinner.''

''Very well, Your Highness.'' Carlos bowed and disappeared through the doorway, only to return promptly with a wheeled cart. He worked efficiently and quietly, whisking a linen tablecloth and napkins from the cart to cover a mahogany table near the back of the cabin. He took silverware from one of the cart's compartments, china and stemware from another, and in moments, the table was set, food steaming on the plates.

He bowed and pushed the cart out of the cabin, closing the door behind him.

Emily, who had watched the steward's transformation of game table to dinner table, glanced at Lazhar. "Is Carlos a genie in his off-hours? Because that was quite a trick."

Lazhar returned her smile. "He's very good at his job." He stood and held out his hand. "Shall we?" Emily took his hand and let him draw her to her feet. "He's worked for my father, and now me, for over twenty years. I followed him around as a child when our family traveled, trying to uncover his secret for producing food at the precise moment my parents wanted it, but I never did. The only thing I ever managed to learn was that he's amazingly organized."

Lazhar pulled out a chair and seated her before taking his own seat across from her.

"This looks wonderful." Determined to maintain a polite, professional distance between them, Emily picked up her fork and took a bite. The grilled fish was crisp on the outside, perfectly cooked on the inside. She sampled the paella as well, the flavors of saffron, red and green peppers blending with shrimp and mussels in a mouthwatering combination. ''It tastes even better than it looks.''

''I'm glad you're pleased. I'll pass your comments on to Carlos.''

They chatted easily during dinner. Lazhar seemed more than willing to answer her questions about his country and the customs that would impact the royal wedding. He had a wry sense of humor that had her laughing and his insightful comments about the differing economic stratas in his country made her realize that he wasn't a prince who isolated himself in a luxurious castle. He must spend a lot of time working alongside the residents of Daniz, she thought as he related a story about attending a rural wedding of a distant cousin. The wedding celebration continued for a week and during that time, the male guests helped erect a small house for the newlyweds. It was clear that Lazhar relished the physical activity of pounding nails and raising walls.

Their dinner long finished, their dessert plates empty and the bottle of wine drained, they remained at the table, Emily listening with fascination to his stories about life in Daniz. *I could care too much for this man,* she realized as she gazed at him, his features animated when he described how the guests had carried his cousin and his bride around the house on their shoulders before leaving them inside the finished structure.

"We'll drive out to the country and visit my cousin and his wife while you're in Daniz," Lazhar commented, glancing at his watch and lifting an eyebrow in surprise. "It's late. I'm afraid I've been boring you with family stories."

"No, not at all." Emily glanced at her own small diamond-studded watch and was shocked to find that it was after midnight. "I had no idea it was this late."

"You should try to get some sleep." He stood and once again, held out his hand. "The bag Jane packed for you is in the bedroom."

Emily put her hand in his, palm against palm, her fingers sliding against his rougher, larger ones. She was getting accustomed to having him take her hand, she realized, and for some reason, didn't mind it. There was something about him that found its way past her defenses and instilled confidence, generating acceptance.

He showed her to a beautifully decorated bedroom off the main cabin and left her with a polite good-night. A wave of weariness hit Emily as she closed and locked the door, her gaze searching the room. Her suitcase sat atop a luggage rack next to the bed and she pulled out her pajamas and toiletry bag, quickly preparing for bed. She was so tired she barely noted the opulent fittings of the bath and bedroom before she turned out the light and slipped between the silk sheets. Within seconds, she was sound asleep.

Their landing and transfer from the plane to the black Mercedes limousine waiting for them the next morning was smooth and effortless. The driver left the airport by a private gate, nosing the big car into busy morning traffic along a wide avenue. Seated next to Lazhar in the back, Emily was entranced by glimpses of the azure sea as they passed narrow side streets leading from the vehicle-choked avenue down to the Daniz Harbor. The limousine made a sharp turn and she caught her breath as they plunged down one such street, so narrow that oncoming vehicles nearly brushed door handles.

"Don't worry," Lazhar said, his deep voice amused. "Antonio has driven this route a thousand times and never so much as scratched the paint."

Emily's gaze left the colorful scene outside her window and glanced at him to find him watching her, an understanding smile curving his lips. A reluctant smile lifted the corner of her mouth in response. "I thought I was accustomed to narrow streets and steep hills," she commented, gesturing at the window beside him. "But San Francisco didn't prepare me for this."

He chuckled. "This part of Daniz City is built

on a series of hills that march up from the harbor
and since it's been here for centuries, the streets
weren't built to accommodate automobiles. I'm accustomed to it since I've lived here all my life, but
I warn visitors that they should think twice before
hiring a car and driving here." He paused, his gaze
intent on her face. "What do you think of my
city?"

"It's beautiful." Her voice sounded as enchanted as she felt. Their car stopped at an inter-
section, waiting for a crowd of strolling pedestrians
to cross the street in front of them, and Emily
leaned closer to Lazhar, the better to see out the
side window. A carpet with a pattern worked in
deep burgundies and rose-reds hung outside the
shop on the corner, its lush colors vibrant against
the pink-tinged stones of the building behind it.
The shop door set into the heavy medieval archway
stood open and Emily caught a glimpse of an Alad-
din's cave of brilliant color before the car moved
forward, leaving the shop behind.

They drove past an open-air market, flowers and
fruit making brilliant splashes of color against the
ancient stone walls laced with black ironwork balconies above.

"You're sincere about finding my city beautiful."

It was a statement, not a question, and when
Emily drew her gaze from the view outside the

window to look at Lazhar, his expression held a quiet pride and satisfaction.

"Yes, it's absolutely fascinating."

They shared a spontaneous smile of accord and for one brief moment, she felt as if she'd known him forever, that he understood exactly how much she enjoyed this glimpse of his city, so very different from her native San Francisco despite both being built on steep hills. Then he glanced away from her and out the window, pointing out the fountain in the center of the square they were currently circling, and the moment was gone.

Emily's first view of the Daniz Royal Palace left her speechless. The castle sat atop a hill, with breathtaking views from all sides. The rose-tinted stone building had medieval square towers with crenellated tops standing guard at each end, the walls connecting the towers lined with high, arched windows on the top two stories, the lower story having only small, square openings covered with glass. It looked like a fortress, which indeed, it had been during its early years.

The limousine smoothly negotiated the winding avenue, lined with Italian poplars and centuries-old buildings housing apartments above and shops at street level. Then they passed through impressive wrought-iron gates manned by uniformed guards to enter the palace grounds. Lush green lawns dotted with huge, century-old trees edged the driveway leading to the palace itself; the car swept to a stop on the cobblestone circular driveway before an imposing door.

The driver and bodyguard immediately exited and held open the door for Lazhar, who handed out Emily, turning away for a moment to converse in low tones with the guard.

Emily's fascinated gaze swept the castle facade, drinking in the sight of stone sculptures carved above each of the many windows and what seemed to be a hanging garden halfway down the building's length, one floor up where a stone balustrade topped the first level.

"Sorry to keep you waiting," Lazhar took her arm and they walked toward the doorway.

Emily barely had time to note the coat of arms carved into the stone above the arched doorway, the two snarling panthers holding crossed swords over a crown. Then they were inside, crossing an entryway tiled with a blue and gold mosaic pattern; the room was easily large enough to hold several hundred people.

"Antonio is taking your bag to your room," Lazhar told her as they ascended one side of the curving staircase to the second floor. "My mother and sister always need to rest after flying home from the States due to the jet lag. When you're ready, your maid will tell you where to find me and we'll discuss the itinerary for your stay."

"Very well," Emily murmured. She caught glimpses into rooms off the hallway that were decorated in a mix of Mediterranean architecture, Persian carpets, Italian glass, French furniture, and Moroccan pillows. She was charmed by the beautiful building with it's jewel-box rooms; somehow the interiors she saw managed to combine palatial elegance with the warmth of a real home.

"Here we are." Lazhar pushed open a door and halted. "If there's anything you want or need that you don't find, please don't hesitate to ask."

"Thank you." Emily stepped into the room, her gaze quickly sweeping the lovely furnishings before she turned to look at him, her fingers closing over the door handle. "You're very kind."

"Not at all." He shrugged, his lashes narrowing as he assessed her. "You look ready to fall asleep standing there. Get some sleep," he said abruptly. "We'll talk after you've rested." And he reached out and caught the edge of the door, gently moving it out of her grasp, closing it between them.

Left alone, Emily surveyed her room and realized that it was actually a suite of rooms. The ruby-and-cream Persian carpet was thick and plush beneath her feet as she walked across the airy sitting room to peek through an open door. Here, the drapes were partially drawn across floor-to-ceiling windows, barring the hot sunlight from the interior. The wide bed was draped in sheer white panels, the pale lemon sheet and green silk coverlet turned back invitingly below the embroidered pillows. Despite the effects of jet lag that had her yawning, Emily walked to the archway and stepped out into a lovely garden. Walled on three sides for privacy with bougainvillea spilling hot pink flowers over the sand-colored stones, the garden was a riot of white and pink roses, fragrant lavender, sage, rosemary and silvery artemisia. One wall was only waist-high and the view of Daniz Harbor and the Mediterranean Sea beyond was breathtaking. Emily drew a deep breath. The tang of salt carried by a faint breeze from the harbor mingled with the sweet scent of the garden's floribunda roses. The breath turned into a yawn and she reluctantly turned away from the spellbinding view of sea and garden to reenter the bedroom. She showered, pulled on a nightgown, and climbed into bed.

She fell asleep the moment her head hit the pillow.

When she woke, the midafternoon sun was slanting through the half-open drapes. Disoriented, she stared at the ceiling for a long moment, wondering why it was a pale rose instead of the eggshell-white she normally saw when waking in her bed in San Francisco.

Because I'm not home in San Francisco. She sat up, pushed her hair out of her eyes, and stared around her. The airy, shaded room was exotic and opulent, a mix of architecture that reflected the countries and cultures that bordered Daniz. The Spanish archway leading to the sitting room was edged with Greek tiles in green and gold and the French influence was apparent in the delicate Louis XIV chair placed in one corner near her bed. An exquisite Italian vase of handblown glass stood on the dresser, its shade of deep green a perfect foil for the white roses and trailing greenery it held. And the high ceilings and airy hangings tied back on the bed, that matched the sheer white draperies at the windows, reminded Emily that Morocco was just across the Mediterranean Sea.

It was so lovely and so exotically different from her apartment in San Francisco that she felt transported into another world.

It is another world, she reminded herself. *The royal palace in a foreign country is definitely light years away from my apartment in San Francisco.*

She tossed back the silky sheet and light coverlet and rose, wondering what time it was and how long she'd slept. She picked up her watch from the nightstand.

"Two o'clock? How could I have slept so long?" she murmured, dismayed that the day was half gone. She hurried into the bathroom where she found herself pausing once again to stare with pleasure at the effect of green and cream tiles, thick cream-colored turkish towels, and pale jade marble tub and sink. It wasn't that she was unaccustomed to the beauty and comfort that money could provide. She'd grown up in her father's opulent mansion; her playmates and friends all lived in similar wealthy homes. But there was something subtly different about Lazhar's home. The deep jewel tones of the carpets were softly muted as if they had covered the teak and marble floors for years. The paintings of ladies and gentleman that hung on the walls bore a resemblance to one another and Emily suspected that they were Lazhar's ancestors. The furnishings spoke of centuries of wealth and history yet conveyed a welcoming warmth that she'd never felt in her father's oddly sterile mansion.

Emily shook herself out of her reverie and turned on the shower faucets, stripping quickly and stepping into the tiled surround.

A half hour later, showered, hair blown dry, makeup applied, wearing only a towel she walked back into the bedroom and halted abruptly. A maid dressed in a soft royal-blue uniform edged in gold, was just setting a tray with teapot and scones atop the small table near the window.

"Good afternoon." Her soft voice was friendly and polite, the English words faintly accented with a musical lilt.

"Hello." Emily glanced at the very English teapot with its pink tea rose pattern. *Yet another country heard from,* she thought.

The maid opened a door to a walk-in closet. "I unpacked your bag this morning and hung your dresses in here." She pulled open a drawer. "And I folded your lingerie into the drawers." She looked expectantly at Emily. "Would you like me to help you dress, ma'am?"

"I think I can manage but thank you for unpacking my things."

"You're very welcome," the young woman murmured. "When you're dressed, I'll show you to the breakfast room."

"Thank you."

The maid smiled and left the room.

Emily waited until the door closed behind her before walking into the closet. She recognized only three of the many dresses and suits that hung on the long rod suspended along one wall. The closet was filled with gowns and casual wear, shoes on racks against the end wall, lingerie tucked into the drawers fitted against the opposite wall from the dress rack. She flipped through a row of dresses, noting the designer labels, before pulling open the drawers to glance at the filmy lingerie, all in her size. The clothing and underpinnings were gorgeous but Emily was torn between appreciation for the beautiful clothing and sheer annoyance that Lazhar obviously knew her measurements, right down to her bra and panties.

Was it possible that he'd ordered an entire wardrobe just for her? *No,* she thought, discounting the idea. That was a grand gesture that a very rich man might make for a potential lover, not for a business associate.

Still, he'd clearly noticed some things about her since he'd guessed her measurements perfectly.

Unless Jane told him, she thought. Emily resolved to have another serious talk with Jane about her role in aiding Lazhar's high-handed methods when she returned to San Francisco.

Chapter Three

Emily followed the maid through unfamiliar halls until the young woman halted, pulled open a door and bowed.

"Prince Lazhar is here, madam."

"Thank you," Emily murmured, and was rewarded with a warm smile from the maid before she stepped across the threshold and the door closed silently behind her.

Lazhar sat at a round table, documents spread across the snowy cloth next to his coffee cup. He looked up as she entered the small dining room, a swift smile curving his mouth, his gaze heating as it flicked over her from head to toe and back again. "Good afternoon, Emily, did you sleep well?"

"Yes, very well, thank you." Emily sat down in the chair held by a white-coated male servant and murmured a thank you when he poured coffee from a carafe into her cup.

"And your room is satisfactory?"

"More than satisfactory." She smiled at him. "The view of the harbor is amazing, as is the garden off the bedroom. Do all the rooms have walled gardens?"

"Many of them, yes." Lazhar dropped the document he was holding and lounged in his chair, nodding at the servant who immediately filled his coffee cup. "The palace gardens are my mother's pride and joy. She'll be pleased you're enjoying her babies."

"Her babies?" Emily looked up from the ruby-red marmalade she was spreading on her toast.

"That's what my mother calls the gardens. She told my sister and me that since we haven't given her grandchildren, she's making do with plants as a substitute for babies." His smile flashed, white against tanned skin, his eyes warming with quick affection. "She's as anxious as my father to see us happily married and starting our own families."

"And do you and your sister agree with her?" Emily asked, curious.

He shrugged. "I can understand our parents'

wish to see us happily settled—especially since my father's health is uncertain. Jenna, however..." He shook his head, amused. "My sister is adamant that she won't be nudged into marrying before she's ready."

"So there's no fiancé waiting in the wings for your sister?"

"No. But it's not for lack of trying by my father."

Emily couldn't help but smile with sympathy. "It hadn't occurred to me before, but I suppose I should be grateful that while my father tries to control my life in other ways, he's never nagged me about getting married—" She broke off, leaning back to let the silent servant place a plate with salmon quiche on the table before her and didn't see the fleeting expression of regret on Lazhar's face. The quiche was every bit as delicious as the sweet cantaloupe and honeydew melon cubes in a small bowl next to her plate. She wondered idly if the family chef would be preparing the wedding food before she remembered that she needed to speak to Lazhar about the designer wardrobe hanging in her bedroom. "Speaking of being grateful..." She glanced up at him to find him watching her, his dark eyes enigmatic. "I noticed that the closet in my room is filled with clothing," she said carefully.

"I asked Mother to have her assistant stock the

closet for you—it seemed only fair since I didn't give you time to pack your own things before we left San Francisco,'' he said smoothly.

How clever of him, she thought, her gaze never leaving his as she slowly sipped water from a chilled Waterford crystal glass. *If I object, then I've insulted his mother. Very clever, indeed.* She returned the glass to the table. ''Please convey my thanks to your mother,'' she said, her voice purposely neutral. ''That was very kind of her.''

''I'll be happy to,'' he replied.

His words were as carefully polite as hers had been, but the amused glint in his dark eyes told her that he knew very well that she was uncomfortable with the situation. The clothing and lingerie were all the right size and that he had guessed so accurately made her painfully aware that he was far too familiar with the female body in general and hers in particular. The undercurrent of sexual tension that stretched between them stole her breath. *He's getting married soon,* she told herself, unable to look away from the heat in his eyes. *It's crazy to feel so attracted to him.* Lecturing herself didn't make her heart stop pounding against her ribcage, nor did it cool the warmth moving slowly through her veins.

''Your Highness?''

Lazhar's gaze left hers, moving past her to the doorway. ''Yes?''

"King Abbar would like you and Miss Parks to join him in his garden this afternoon."

"Very well. Tell him we'll be with him shortly." The servant bowed and left the room and Lazhar once again focused his attention on Emily. "I hope you don't mind postponing our discussion of your itinerary until later. My father mentioned earlier that he wanted to meet you and since he must spend much of his time resting, we all tend to adjust our schedules to fit his."

"That's perfectly understandable—I'd be delighted to meet the king." Emily glanced at her plate and realized that while she'd struggled to cope with the sexual tension between them, she'd mindlessly continued to fork food into her mouth and her plate was empty. She barely remembered chewing and swallowing. Annoyed that Lazhar had distracted her to such an extent, she blotted her lips with her napkin and placed the linen square neatly beside her plate. "I'm ready."

Lazhar didn't comment but again she caught the gleam of amusement in his eyes as he stood and held her chair.

They left the dining room and by the time they made a right and then a left turn down wide hallways, Emily was completely confused.

"Has a guest ever gotten lost in the palace?" she asked as they passed an open doorway and she caught a quick glimpse of a sitting room, tastefully decorated in feminine rose and pink shades.

"Often, but never for long. See the gold corded ropes hanging next to every third door?"

"Yes." Emily hadn't noticed them before.

"They're bell-pulls connected to the main housekeeping office. If you're ever lost, just tug on one of them and a speaker hidden in the wall above the door will allow you to ask directions from one of the staff."

"That's very ingenious."

"Mother thought of it. I wanted to tie the speakers into the security system with the cameras but she thought it was too intrusive. She didn't want guests reminded that they're being watched, particularly here in our family quarters." Lazhar paused outside mahogany double doors carved with the Daniz coat-of-arms. The two palace guards flanking the doors snapped to attention, saluted, and pulled open the heavy doors.

They crossed the threshold and Emily's eyes widened as her gaze swept the expansive apartment. The white marble floor was partially covered by scattered Persian carpets in the royal colors of deep blue and gold. The room seemed more Eastern than European with its low blue sofas, mahogany tables, and large blue and gold silk pillows piled on the floor. One whole wall was glass with transparent white panels of silk drawn over half the length to deflect the brilliant, hot sunshine pouring into the high-ceilinged space. Emily caught her breath as they crossed the room and stepped through open doors into the garden beyond. The walled garden was bigger, more lush than the one outside her suite of rooms but it was the view beyond the waist-high stone balustrade that halted her. Not only were the harbor and the city's red-tiled roofs visible but also the pine and cypress covered hills above Daniz City's narrow streets. The king's garden boasted a one-hundred-and-eighty-degree view of mountains, harbor, sea and city that was so impressive that for a moment, Emily didn't notice that she and Lazhar weren't alone in the garden.

"Ah, Lazhar, is this lovely young woman our guest from San Francisco?"

"Yes, Father, this is Emily."

Startled from her absorption, Emily realized that Lazhar had been standing silently, waiting for her attention, and that an older man sat on a cushioned chaise lounge at the far end of the garden, shaded by the wide, leafy branches of an acacia tree. "I'm so sorry," she apologized, embarrassment heating her cheeks. "I'm being terribly rude, please forgive me." She gestured at the panoramic view. "You have such an amazing view."

Lazhar cupped her elbow and escorted her the length of the garden to the small semicircle of chairs arranged beneath the spreading branches of the tree.

"Emily, I'd like you to meet my father, King Abbar."

"It's a pleasure to meet you, sir." Emily wasn't sure if she should curtsy but before she could decide, the king gestured at the wrought-iron cushioned chairs next to his lounge.

"Please, join me."

Emily felt the king's shrewd gaze assessing her as Lazhar seated her next to his father and took the chair beside her.

"I'm pleased you find my country interesting," the king continued.

"What I've seen so far has been fascinating," Emily confided, charmed by the friendly warmth in the king's dark eyes. Despite the sun, his skin had the pallor of ill health and his thin body seemed fragile; nevertheless the family connection between father and son was readily apparent. This is what Lazhar will look like when he's older, she thought, taking in the bone structure and keen nearly black eyes, the boyish grin that curved his mouth as he nodded with approval at her comment, his assessing gaze developing a distinct twinkle. Like his son, he had an air of masculine elegance, though his white jacket, shirt and pale-gray slacks were much more casual than Lazhar's gray suit.

"You must take her to the Jewel Market, Lazhar.'' King Abbar's gaze turned thoughtful as he glanced from his son to Emily. ''Or perhaps you have already seen the Market, Emily? I understand that your father has been involved in gem trading for many years.''

''Since before I was born,'' Emily confirmed. ''He and my brother have visited the Market here in Daniz, but I haven't had the pleasure.''

''Your father didn't take the family with him on business trips?'' the king asked, waving a servant closer to pour coffee for his guests.

''No. He doesn't believe in mixing business with family matters.'' Emily smiled her thanks as she took a delicate cup and saucer from the young man serving her. She didn't see the questioning glance King Abbar gave Lazhar, nor the slight shake of his son's head in response. ''We didn't travel with him at all. In fact, I've never been out of the States until last night.''

''Never?'' Lazhar's surprise was evident.

''Never—except for short trips across the U.S. border into Mexico and Canada and I don't count those since they're our neighboring countries.'' She sipped her coffee, the sweet, strong brew foreign to her tongue. ''Not that I didn't want to travel,'' she said hastily as she glanced up to find the king's dark gaze assessing her. ''I planned to take a year off and tour Europe after college, but then I had the opportunity to start Creative Weddings and I decided to postpone a European tour until later. Since then, I've focused on building the business and any traveling I managed to squeeze in has been to visit clients in the U.S. I can't seem to get away from the office for longer than a day or two.''

''Then we're fortunate that you've taken this time to spend with us,'' the king said. ''I understand that you've agreed to plan Lazhar's wedding.''

''I'm very interested in the possibility,'' Emily said carefully. ''As I told your son, however, I won't be able to put together a comprehensive proposal until I've seen the facilities, talked to your staff, and have a bit more input from him, his fiancée, and your family.''

The king waved away her concerns. ''I'm certain that your proposal will be acceptable. My son has chosen you and I have complete confidence in his judgment in this matter. Even more so now that I've met you.'' His eyes twinkled.

''Thank you, Father,'' Lazhar said wryly.

This is how it should be between a father and son, Emily thought, as the two exchanged a look of complete understanding. Seeing Lazhar with his father made Emily realize why he had spirited her out of San Francisco and what made him willing to do whatever it took to make his father's wish a reality. He clearly loved his father and even Emily, who had never felt that mutual affection between herself and her father, couldn't help but recognize the depth of the connection between the two.

"I told Emily that she needs to tour the country and meet our people in order to understand more about Danizian culture before creating a wedding plan," Lazhar continued.

"An excellent idea." The king nodded in agreement. "And you'll be her guide, of course—where will you begin?"

"I thought we'd dine at the palace this evening, with mother and Jenna. Emily can sample traditional Daniz recipes and the work of the chef who will be preparing the food for the reception and wedding banquet. After dinner, we'll tour the casino." He looked at Emily. "Unless there's something else you'd prefer to do this evening?"

Emily shook her head. "Not at all, it sounds like an excellent plan."

The king glanced at his watch. "I'm sure you'll enjoy both our chef's dinner and the casino, Emily. And now, I'm afraid I must say good afternoon. I have another appointment that I must keep."

Emily rose, waiting while Lazhar helped his father to his feet before the king took the arm of a burly manservant. The white clad servant had appeared so silently that Emily was unaware he was near until he stepped forward to hold out his arm for the king to lean on.

"Good afternoon, Emily." The king held out his free hand. "I'm very glad you've come to stay with us."

"Thank you." Emily took his hand in hers, surprised by the strength in the thin fingers. Although he was as tall as his son, King Abbar seemed almost frail in comparison to Lazhar and the stocky servant. An indomitable spirit and will blazed from his eyes but it was clear that the king was ill.

"We will talk again tomorrow."

"I look forward to it."

The king smiled with approval and turned to his son. "Come to my rooms before you go down to dinner, Lazhar. There is something I wish to discuss with you."

"Of course, Father."

Emily stood silently beside Lazhar, watching the king's labored steps as he left the garden with his aide and disappeared through a door at the far end of the patio.

"Your father is a very charming man," Emily commented as Lazhar walked beside her to reenter the high-ceilinged living room. "The two of you seem very close."

"We're father and son," Lazhar said simply, opening the door to the hall. Again, the guards snapped to attention.

"So are Cade and my father, but I've never thought of their relationship as anything but...

distant.'' ''Difficult,'' or even ''adversarial'' might better describe the association between her brother and Walter, she thought, but years of listening to her father's commands forbidding any discussions about the family with outsiders made her choose a milder word.

''That's unfortunate.'' Lazhar paused outside a door and Emily realized that he'd returned her to her suite. ''My father and I have grown closer since I became an adult and took over our national security. But even when I was a child and he was busy with the grueling job of running the country, with a thousand daily demands on his time, he always insisted that we share meals together as a family and each evening, he and mother tucked us in bed.'' A fond smile quirked his mouth. ''They're both very hands-on parents. How about you, Emily?'' he asked softly, his gaze focused intently on hers. ''Do you want children? Do you see yourself as a mother who insists on tucking them in each night? Or would you leave them to nannies and governesses?''

''No governesses.'' Emily shook her head. ''And no nannies.''

''You say that with great conviction,'' he commented.

''I was raised by my father's housekeeper. Brenda is a wonderful woman and we were very lucky to have her, but children should have their parents involved in their lives." Realizing that she may have revealed more than she intended, Emily shrugged and tried for a careless tone. "But I probably won't have children, so it's a nonissue for me."

He lifted an eyebrow, folded his arms across his chest and leaned his shoulder against the wall. "You don't plan to have children? You don't look forward to marrying?"

He looked as if he had all the time in the world to discuss her marital status, or lack of one. Emily almost groaned out loud. Why had she been so adamant about methods of parenting children? Granted, she felt very strongly about the issue, but she needed to keep Lazhar at arm's length. His affection and care for his father had already melted some of the barriers she'd erected around her emotions. She didn't want to discuss her feelings about children with him. What if he were understanding and kind? *Excellent qualities if I were his fiancée because they would make me love him more,* she thought, *but since I'm only the wedding planner and a business associate, not so good for me to know.*

"I have a company to run," she said lightly. "I don't have time to think about children, certainly not for the foreseeable future."

"But someday, you plan to marry and have children," he prodded.

"I doubt it." Something about him compelled her to be truthful when she'd planned to be evasive. She couldn't bring herself to lie outright to him.

"That would be a terrible waste," he said quietly. His gaze left hers and stroked over her face, lightly grazing her lips with an almost tangible touch. He brushed a strand of hair from her cheek and tucked it behind her ear. "You'll have beautiful children, Emily, and you'll make a wonderful mother. You have a soft heart and good instincts."

His deep voice thrummed along Emily's veins, making her blood move more swiftly. His dark gaze held hers and Emily felt her bones melting, her body swaying toward his where he leaned against the wall.

The murmur of voices, growing louder as they moved nearer down the hall, snapped Emily back to awareness. She flushed. Lazhar's fingers trailed across her hot cheek before his hand fell away and he pushed away from the wall to open the door behind her.

"Dinner's at eight. I'll be back to take you to the dining room. I wouldn't want you getting lost."

Emily murmured a thank-you and stepped inside, closing the door and sagging against it for support because her legs felt like rubber.

Lazhar Eban is a dangerous man. She moved

away from the door. *I bet every woman he meets falls in love with him. But not me—I can't afford to care about him. I'm only here to plan his wedding.* She shook her head at her reflection in the wall-to-wall mirror over the bathroom vanity. Her cheeks were flushed, her eyes dark, and to her dismay, her nipples were clearly visible, pushing against the white silk blouse she wore under the jacket of her yellow linen suit.

Damn. She groaned and turned away from the woman in the mirror. Lazhar would have noticed, he'd been standing too close, his attention too focused on her, and he was too male to have missed the obvious signs of arousal.

She stripped off her clothes and turned the shower jets on, determined to have a better grip on her emotions during dinner and the planned visit to the Daniz Casino.

Lazhar knocked at his father's open bedroom door later that evening.

''Come in.''

King Abbar was in bed. The huge mahogany bedstead had blue silk hangings, tied back with gold cord against the four heavy posts at each corner. The headboard was carved with the royal crest and a dozen fat white pillows cushioned the king's back against the wood. The pillow shams, sheets, blankets and bedskirt were all white. The king preferred plain over opulent and while he'd left the rest of the palace's historical decorations intact, he'd stripped his own bedchamber of all gilt and velvet the moment he ascended to the throne. The result was a room that was supremely comfortable and reflected the king's masculine practicality.

"Good evening, Father. How are you feeling?"

"I'm well, all things considered."

Lazhar acknowledged the king's dry comment with a half smile as he walked across the room. Despite his father's constant reassurances, he knew that each day was a struggle. He searched the lined face and saw the weariness in the droop of eyelids and the slump of thin shoulders once military straight. "Are you sure you want to talk? I can come back in the morning after you're rested."

"I'm tired, but that's nothing new. Don't fuss, Lazhar, I get enough of that from your mother. Sit, sit." Abbar gestured at the chair next to the bed, but didn't wait for Lazhar to drop into it before he continued. "I like your Emily. I confess I had doubts when you told me that you'd chosen Walter Parks's daughter as your bride, but I was most pleasantly surprised when I met her today. She's nothing like her father. In fact, I quite liked her."

Tension that Lazhar hadn't realized existed eased at his father's words. Relieved, he crossed one ankle over the opposite knee, leaned back in the chair, and chuckled. "I thought you would. And no, she's definitely nothing like her father."

"The connection with Walter Parks may turn out to be more of a problem than an asset. Are you sure you want to be involved in business dealings with him? He has a reputation for ruthlessness among the gem traders."

"I can handle him."

"What about the rumors that he's been involved in illegal activity? I read the newspaper articles you faxed me from San Francisco and I have to wonder whether Parks is a company we should associate ourselves with."

"What I learned about Parks while I was in San Francisco leads me to believe that the company is strong, but that Walter Parks may have reached the end of what could be a dirty career path. I had the impression that what was printed in the newspaper might be just the tip of the iceberg."

The king pursed his lips, his gaze shrewd. "And in spite of those problems, you don't think a business association between Daniz and his company will tarnish our reputation?"

"No. The deal is airtight and I've had every aspect of the contract details checked. Walter Parks's personal life may self-destruct, but the Parks company won't, certainly not in the mining venture that we'll be involved in."

"Very well. Does Emily know about the connection between you and her father?"

"No, and I don't want her to until I'm ready to tell her."

"And when will that be?"

"I don't know yet."

The king shook his head. "She doesn't appear to be the kind of woman who will easily forgive being lied to."

"I'm not lying to her. I've never told her I *didn't* know her father."

"*Hmph.* Perhaps not. But you're lying by omission when you purposely keep silent because you know that the acquaintance would affect how she feels about you."

"You're probably right," Lazhar admitted reluctantly. "I plan to tell her, but not until we know each other better. If I tell her now that I'm considering joining her father in a gem mining operation, she'll write me off as just another of her father's business associates obsessed with jewels. I need time."

"Then you'd better hope that she doesn't learn the truth before you tell her." Abbar considered his son for a moment. "What made you choose Emily over all the other women you know? You hadn't met her before this week, had you?"

"No. I've been to San Francisco on business more than once but our paths never crossed at any of the gem market functions and after hearing her comments about how she views the industry, I'm not surprised. I doubt she attended very many jewel conferences.''

''So you literally had never seen her until Walter Parks sent her photo to you?''

''No, I'd never seen her.''

''What was it about her picture that was so intriguing?'' King Abbar's voice was mildly curious.

Lazhar shrugged. ''She's a very beautiful woman.''

''True,'' the king agreed. ''But there are many beautiful women in the world. And if gossip can be believed, you've dated several hundred.''

Lazhar's gaze sharpened, scanning his father's face. ''Gossip? Who's been telling you tales?''

Abbar waved a hand dismissingly. ''No one important. Don't worry, Lazhar, I'm aware that you've been very circumspect about the women you've associated with since college. But that doesn't mean I don't know their names, or that I haven't seen them, either in photos or in person.''

Lazhar shook his head, a slight smile tugging the corners of his mouth upward. ''You have eyes and ears everywhere.''

''Yes,'' Abbar said mildly. ''I'm the king, it's my job to know these things. And since I'm well aware of the long list of women friends you have,

I'm even more curious as to why, out of all the women you know, you chose Emily Parks?''

"Besides the fact that she's beautiful, well-educated and socially adept so she can cope with the responsibilities of being part of our family, Walter made marriage to her part of his business proposal.''

"Marrying solely to gain an edge in a business deal doesn't sound wise, Lazhar.'' A frown wrinkled Abbar's forehead.

"That's not the only reason,'' Lazhar said dryly. "I suppose I should admit that I took one look at her picture and wanted to bed her. That didn't change once I'd met her, in fact, it's grown stronger.''

"Ah.'' The two exchanged a very male look of understanding. "Perhaps not the single best reason for marrying, but certainly important.'' Abbar's shrewd gaze studied Lazhar. "Did you reach any other conclusions about your Emily when you met her face-to-face that convinced you she was the woman you wanted to marry?''

Lazhar had an instant memory of Emily and Walter's housekeeper talking about her yearning for a family. "Yes.'' His gaze met Abbar's. "She wants to marry and have children, but seems to have given up on the possibility. I can give her what she wants and needs, in return, I'll get what I want and need. It's a good bargain.''

"But you haven't told her any of this?"

"Not yet."

"Ah." King Abbar shifted against the pillows. "I think you should find a way to tell her your plans as soon as possible. Women can be unreasonable if they get the misguided impression that we're not consulting their wishes."

Lazhar mentally winced. His father was right, he thought, and Emily already had good cause to be displeased with him after he'd whisked her away from San Francisco without consulting her.

"You're right, Father. I'll tell her as soon as I can think of a way to bring up the subject without causing her to run straight back to San Francisco."

"I think you have your work cut out for you, son," Abbar said with a smile of commiseration.

Lazhar read the growing signs of weariness on his father's face and in the greater slump of his shoulders. He glanced at his watch and stood. "I promised Emily I'd collect her for dinner. I don't want her to get lost." He bent and kissed King Abbar's forehead. "Good night. I'll see you at breakfast."

"Good night, my son."

Emily planned to wear the Vera Wang cocktail dress that evening, the one she'd first donned for dinner with Lazhar in San Francisco. But when she walked into her closet to look for the little black dress, she gave in to temptation and slipped into a sinfully sexy, ankle-length, emerald-green evening gown. The lace-covered bodice was cut straight across the upper curve of her breasts and the short sleeves cupped her shoulders, leaving the long line of her throat and creamy shoulders bare. The dress was a slim, straight tube of emerald lace over satin, slit up the side to her thigh. Emily stared at her reflection in the mirror. She'd owned designer gowns since she was in her teens but she'd never had a dress that made her feel so alive. The color made her eyes glow a deeper, more mysterious green; her hair gleamed with golden highlights under the dressing room lights; her skin smooth and lightly tan against the delicate emerald lace.

I shouldn't, she thought, torn with indecision. *But on the other hand, will the queen be offended if I don't wear the clothes she ordered for me?*

Her conscience was still arguing with her love of pretty clothes when a light rap sounded at the door. The clock on the mantel read seven forty-five.

"You're early," she said as she opened the door for Lazhar and turned to collect her Palm Pilot from the delicate French table just inside the doorway.

"I know," Lazhar acknowledged as she stepped into the hall and he closed the door. "What's this?"

"This?" Emily held up the small electronic day-planner.

"Yes, that."

"It's my planner."

"I know what an electronic day-planner is, Emily, I use one myself. What I don't know is why you're taking it to dinner."

"It's easier to carry than a notepad and pen. If your mother or sister discuss any details they think should be included in your wedding, I can jot down notes so I won't forget."

"Emily," Lazhar halted her by the simple method of closing his hand around her arm. "This is just a casual family dinner. You don't need to take notes."

"But...."

"No buts." He slipped the Palm Pilot out of her hand and tucked it into his jacket pocket. "You can take all the notes you like tomorrow, but for tonight, forget about work, okay? My mother is looking forward to meeting you, and Jenna to seeing you once again."

Emily sighed and gave in. "All right. But if you really want this wedding to take place in six months, then I must start the preliminary work tomorrow. And I need to contact my office first thing in the morning to check with my assistant and verify that she isn't having any problems with clients that I need to resolve since I left without talking to anyone. Early tomorrow, I must get back to work,'' she said firmly as he tucked her hand through his arm and resumed their walk down the corridor.

''Of course,'' he assured her.

But the amused glint in his eyes and the grin he gave her made Emily shake her head. ''Just remember, you're the one who said he wanted a wedding celebration put together in a very short time,'' she said.

''I know. I promise I'll let you take all the notes you want tomorrow.''

An hour later, Emily was thoroughly charmed by the queen, who insisted that Emily call her Caroline, and she was reminded again how much she'd liked Jenna Eban when they'd met at her friend's San Francisco wedding.

''Have you seen Angela since her wedding?'' Emily asked over dessert.

''Twice,'' Jenna nodded. ''She was in Paris with her husband three months ago and I met them there for the weekend. And I flew to San Francisco six months before that to stay with her for a week.''

''And both times she brought home a plane load full of new clothes,'' Lazhar commented, a smile tilting his lips as he sipped his wine.

Jenna shrugged. ''We shopped,'' she admitted. Her dark eyes were bright with mischief. ''It was

Paris and San Francisco, after all, how could we *not* shop?''

"Easily," her brother said. "Your closets were already full. What did you do with all the clothes you must have thrown out to make room for the new ones?"

"I donated them to charity," Jenna replied. "Mother and I packed two boxes and took them to the Sisters of Mercy Hospital for their annual fund-raiser. The nuns were delighted to get them."

"I'm sure they were. I wouldn't be surprised if some of them had never been worn."

"Not true!" Jenna shook her head. "Absolutely not true. I didn't give away anything that I hadn't worn several times."

Caroline smiled at Emily. "Lazhar always teases us about the number of gowns we buy, but we're often photographed and the press has an amazing ability to remember if we wear an outfit more than two or three times." She sighed. "It's a shame, really, because I've had to give up some gowns and suits that I truly loved."

"Except for her Chanel suits." Jenna put in. "She can't bear to part with them."

"They're classics," Caroline said firmly. "And I have to draw the line somewhere. Besides, I really adore those suits."

"It's not easy being a queen," Lazhar said to

Emily, his deep voice filled with affectionate teasing as he grinned at his mother.

"That's true," Caroline said promptly. "Your family is well-known in San Francisco, Emily, and I'm sure the society photographers follow you. Do you have this problem?"

"Very rarely. Now that I'm an adult and no longer live at home, I seldom attend functions with my father. But when he requires the family's appearance at one of the charity dinners or fundraisers that the Parks company supports, I try to make sure I never wear the same dress twice."

"How do you do that?" Jenna asked.

"I taped a list to the inside of my closet door and write down dates, events and what I wear to each one."

"Emily likes to make lists," Lazhar commented.

"I like to be organized," she corrected him calmly, determined to ignore the shiver of attraction she felt each time he smiled at her.

"Mother and I make lists, too," Jenna added. "Except my maid keeps track of what I wore where and when. Mother's secretary keeps a running total for her."

"I have a staff of two terrific women at the office that keep track of my business appointments," Emily commented. "I'd be lost without them."

"It's the same for Jenna and I, as well as Lazhar

and his father. Our commitments to appear at functions on behalf of the crown are a part of our family business," Caroline said. "Without staff to assist us, we'd be hopelessly lost in no time."

"Do royal functions take up all of your time?" Emily asked, curious.

"A great deal of it," Caroline responded. "I always make time to spend with the family, of course. And Jenna has cut back on some of her volunteer work because she's become more involved with the day-to-day running of the palace stables since my husband asked Lazhar to take over as head of Daniz security."

"Mother also spends one day a week at the Sisters of Mercy Hospital," Lazhar said. "Volunteering in the children's ward."

"I trained as a pediatrics nurse before marrying Abbar," Caroline explained to Emily. "And although my other duties make it impossible to have a full-time career outside the palace, I like to keep my hand in at the hospital."

"And she gets to hold the babies." Jenna winked at Emily, a mischievous smile lighting her face. "I think that's the real reason she never misses her time at the hospital."

"Until you and your brother give me grandchildren, I have every intention of cooing at babies in the maternity ward every chance I get."

Jenna rolled her eyes, Lazhar chuckled, and their

mother serenely sipped her coffee, ignoring them both.

Just like an ordinary family, teasing each other over dinner, Emily thought. *Only this family lives in a royal palace and their husband and father is the king.* She found it amazing that they were so warm and approachable. Lazhar was relaxed and open, teasing his younger sister, affectionately attentive to his mother. The cool businessman she'd first met in her San Francisco office was absent, replaced in this private setting by a son and brother who clearly loved his family.

She was having trouble keeping her perspective. It was increasingly difficult to think of Lazhar as a client when everything about him seemed to have been tailor-made to fit her private dream of the perfect man.

He's not perfect, she told herself firmly. *This is the guy that tricked you into boarding a plane and then flew you to a foreign country without first asking your permission.*

A small voice reminded her that Lazhar had an understandable reason for doing so, but she ignored it. She needed reasons to convince her foolish heart that Lazhar wasn't a perfect prince. She'd take what she could get.

Emily was still contemplating the unwise attraction she felt for Lazhar when they left the palace for the Daniz casino. They'd said good-night to

Jenna and Caroline after dessert—Caroline leaving to look in on her husband and Jenna off to join friends at a small birthday party. Emily had hoped Lazhar's sister would join them to provide a buffer between herself and the prince, but Jenna waved goodbye with a promise to see them the next morning.

Fortunately for Emily's peace of mind, Lazhar seemed intent on playing tour guide as the black Mercedes limousine wound through the narrow streets. The city seemed even more exotic and foreign to Emily under cover of night, the narrow streets sometimes shadowed, sometimes brightly lit.

"The casino provides employment for many of our citizens as well as generating income for the monarchy," Lazhar said as they turned a corner onto a wide avenue.

A short block away, the avenue ended in the circular driveway facing the casino.

"It looks like photos I've seen of the Opera House in Paris. Is there a connection?" Enchanted, Emily smiled with delight and looked at Lazhar for confirmation.

"The architect was Charles Garnier, who also designed the Paris Opera House and the Monte Carlo Casino in Monaco." Lazhar leaned closer and his fingertip brushed her cheek, just to the left of the corner of her mouth. "When you smile, you have dimples.'' His voice was distracted, his gaze intent.

Emily forgot to breathe. Warmth lingered where the tip of his finger had touched her. ''I know. You haven't noticed them before?''

''I noticed. But they aren't always there.''

A tiny frown of confusion pleated her brow. ''They aren't?''

''No. Only when you really smile, like you did just now, do they appear.'' His voice was deeper, the smooth tones roughened and faintly uneven.

''I didn't know,'' she murmured, held by the heat in his eyes and the slow, repeated brush of his fingers against the spot near the corner of her mouth. He bent nearer, his big hand cupping her chin, his fingertips gently covering the frantically beating pulse in her throat. He was going to kiss her. Emily desperately wanted him to; her lashes lowered, her gaze fastened on his mouth as he drew closer.

The car stopped moving.

Despite the opaque glass that separated them from the driver and bodyguard in front, Lazhar heard the passenger door open and knew that he had only seconds. He forced his fingers to leave Emily's silky, warm skin and eased away from her. Her lashes lifted and she stared at him, clearly disoriented.

''We're at the casino,'' he murmured, watching

her. The bemusement cleared from her eyes and she glanced over his shoulder just as the door opened behind him.

"So we are." Her cheeks were flushed but her voice was calm, composed.

Lazhar wished he were as cool but frustration tightened his muscles and he had to quell the urge to pull the door shut, take her in his arms and to hell with the crowd gathering outside. Instead, he slid out of the car and turned to hold out his hand to Emily.

The thigh-high slit in her gown's skirt allowed a tantalizing glimpse of shapely leg, ankle and strappy heeled sandals as she took his hand and let him draw her out of the limo. The casino security staff stood in a semicircle, creating an oasis among the elegantly dressed crowd of onlookers.

Someone called to Lazhar and he lifted a hand, smiling with cool ease before tucking Emily's hand through his arm and bending closer. "The security staff will escort us into the casino. Don't worry, just keep walking and smile and wave."

Lightbulbs flashed, excited Danizians and tourists called hellos as they moved quickly across the forecourt and through the wide bronze doors into the casino's huge foyer.

The security staff, each holding a walkie-talkie in their hand and wearing headpieces that allowed them to hear, escorted them across the marble floor to a series of arched doorways.

Emily's eyes widened as they paused at the top of the shallow stairs just past one of the rococo-carved doorways. Before them stretched the main floor of the casino. Carpeted in plush red, with enormous Waterford crystal chandeliers suspended from the domed ceiling, the gaming tables a mix of turn-of-the-century mahogany and state-of-the-art machines, the Daniz Casino was awash in a glittering, shifting crowd of tuxedo-clad men and designer-gowned women.

The air hummed with excitement and tension.

"Oh, this is marvelous. What fun." She turned to Lazhar, smiling with anticipation. "I love it."

"I'm glad you approve." He nearly groaned with frustration. He wondered how long she'd want to play? How long till they would once again be in the dark privacy of the limo and he could touch her again, taste her as he wanted to? "What do you prefer? Cards? Roulette? Dice?"

"I have no idea." She smiled at him again before her fascinated gaze drifted over the scene before them. "I've only been to Las Vegas a couple of times and I tried my hand at blackjack, but only because the friend I was with played."

"Friend?" The swift stab of dark jealousy took Lazhar by surprise.

Chapter Four

"Yes, my friend Jane and I were there for a wedding convention last year." She looked up at him. "You remember Jane, don't you."

Relief washed over him. "Yes, I remember Jane."

"Lazhar?"

The casino manager, his tall lean body elegant in a black tuxedo and a welcoming grin on his swarthy face, strode quickly up the steps from the gambling floor. The guards stepped aside, allowing him to enter the small oasis of space their circle created around the prince and Emily.

"Esteban." Lazhar held out his hand. "How's business this evening?"

The manager's handshake was brief but firm. "The house is doing well, as usual."

"Good to hear. Emily, this is Esteban Garcia, the man who controls the casino. Esteban, this is Emily Parks." Emily was friendly but no more than polite as Esteban bowed over her hand and returned her smile with a glint of male appreciation. She glanced at Lazhar. When she lifted a brow in inquiry, he realized that his jaw was set, his fingers curled into fists and he had the distinct urge to punch Esteban for smiling at her and holding her hand for seconds longer than he thought was necessary.

What the hell is wrong with me? He'd wanted many women, but he'd never before felt this combination of possessiveness and lust.

He flexed his fingers, purposely relaxing tense muscles. "Emily would like to play," he said, his voice bland. "Perhaps the roulette wheel?"

"Certainly." Esteban took one of the handheld walkie-talkies from a guard and spoke into it, his fluent Spanish liquid and musical. He handed the small transmitter back to the guard. "It's arranged. Would you like to play in a private room upstairs or down on the floor?"

Lazhar looked at Emily. She was half-turned away from them, her face animated as she drank in the sight of the colorful crowd shifting under the glittering lights, her gaze following the activity on the casino floor with obvious interest. "Downstairs—I think Emily will enjoy the excitement of the crowd."

"Very good." Esteban gave a quiet command and the guards moved down the shallow, carpeted steps. "If you and Miss Parks will come with me, Lazhar…"

A ripple of excited whispers followed in their wake as the three crossed the huge room, the guards clearing a path in front of them with Lazhar's personal bodyguard following behind.

Lazhar was accustomed to celebrity status and the attention his presence always received. He accepted it as part of the downside of being born into the royal family. But tonight, he was more aware of being the focus of all eyes because of Emily. Would the attention worry her? Annoy her? Scare her? How would she handle it?

He needn't have worried, he realized a few moments later. Emily dealt with the attention with calm serenity. Most of the casino guests were intent on their own gambling, but a small crowd of onlookers gathered around the roulette table where Esteban himself manned the wheel. Lazhar seated Emily on one of the tall, low-backed stools upholstered in red leather and took the seat beside her.

There were four other people at the table, three

men and one woman. The men nodded briefly in greeting, while the woman's gaze flicked assessingly over Emily and lingered for a moment on Lazhar before returning to the wheel on the table in front of them.

"Roulette is easy to learn." Lazhar rested his arm on the back of Emily's chair and leaned close to her, his lips brushing the delicate shell of her ear. "Esteban will give you chips." He gestured at the stack of playing chips on the table in front of each player. "You notice that everyone has different colored chips so the dealer can quickly identify the bets." He nodded at Esteban and the dealer deftly counted and then slid two handfuls of blue chips across the table to Emily. "Now you place your chips on the numbered squares on the table, wherever you'd like."

Emily looked up at him. "How do I know which numbers to choose?"

"Some players have lucky numbers they always play. Some believe in intuition and playing their hunches for the night."

"I don't have a lucky number and my intuition is silent. So how do I pick a number?"

"Tell me the first number that comes into your mind—quick, don't think about it."

"Seven," she said promptly.

"Now another number."

"Twenty-two."

"Okay. Now pick any combination of those numbers between one and thirty-six—add, subtract, whatever—and put chips on those numbers."

She stared at him for a moment, a small smile curving her lips. "Does that work? Will I win?"

He shrugged. "I have no idea. It was my grandfather's system and he swore that it worked for him."

"That's good enough for me." She looked at the table with interest and carefully placed chips on seven, twenty-two, and twenty-nine. Then she paused, studying the table, half-turning to murmur. "Why are some of the chips sitting directly on top of the numbers, and some placed at the corners?"

"The ones on the corners are 'corner bets'—the bet covers the four numbers that join at the corner where the chip sits." He nodded at the black and red squares numbered from one to thirty-six and her blue chip resting squarely in the center of number twenty-two. "Your bet on number twenty-two is called a 'straight bet'—the ball has to stop on the wheel at twenty-two in order for you to win."

"Hmmm," Emily tapped the tip of her forefinger against her chin and considered the table. "Which bet has the best odds?"

"The straight bet—the odds are thirty-five to one."

"Then I'll stay with that." She smiled at him, the elusive dimple at the corner of her mouth appearing and disappearing in a flash. "If I win, I win big."

"True." Amused at the risk-taker attitude in Emily when he'd mostly seen her exhibit cool, calm control up until now, Lazhar nodded at Esteban.

The dealer acknowledged him with a barely perceptible nod in return. "Bets down, ladies and gentlemen." The other players around the table nodded and Esteban spun the wheel in one direction and the small silver ball in the other. The ball left the track, rolling onto the spinning wheel. "No more bets!"

The ball bounced and moved, coming to rest in a black compartment of the wheel.

"Black twenty-nine." Esteban called out.

Emily clapped her hands with glee. "I won!" She looked up at Lazhar. "I did win, didn't I?"

"Yes, you definitely won," he said dryly, exchanging an amused glance with Esteban as the dealer stacked a large pile of chips in front of her.

Emily's eyes rounded. "I won all that?"

"The odds were thirty-five to one." He grinned at her. "You wanted to win big, remember?"

"I remember." She flashed him a wide smile. "This is fun." She watched the other gamblers at the table as Esteban either deftly swept away their lost chips, or paid out their wins. Each of them instantly returned chips to the table.

"Should I pick the same numbers, or different ones?"

"Your choice. What do you want to do?"

"I think I'll use the same numbers." Emily put chips on the numbers she'd chosen for the first round. Then she took three chips from her winnings, stacked them neatly on top of the original pile that Esteban had given her, and moved them aside.

"What are you doing?"

"I'm playing with the money I won and leaving the original chips alone. That way," Emily explained, "when I lose the chips I've won, I'll know it's time to stop playing. If I mix the two piles together, I'm afraid I won't remember what the original investment was."

Surprised, Lazhar searched her earnest expression.

"What?" A tiny frown pleated her forehead between her brows and he smoothed it away with his fingertip. Faint pink color bloomed on her cheeks and throat.

"I'm impressed," he said softly, his gaze holding hers as Esteban set the wheel and ball in motion and announced no more bets.

"Why?"

"Because very few people are wise enough to play with the house's money and not theirs. Especially not when they're new to gambling—they usually get swept up in the excitement and lose track of the amount of money they're investing."

Emily glanced at the stack of blue chips. "How much money am I investing?" she asked, curious.

"Red seven," Esteban announced.

"This is a hundred-dollar table," Lazhar said casually.

"A hundred dollars?" Her gaze flicked from him to the table, where Esteban was once again collecting from the losers and paying the winners. He deposited a stack of chips in front of Emily and she looked at Lazhar. "Are you telling me that each of the chips I'm playing with is worth a hundred dollars?"

"Yes."

"That means I've won—" she quickly calculated "—seven thousand dollars?"

"That sounds right." He chuckled at her stunned expression.

"But what if I'd lost?"

He shrugged. "You wouldn't have seven thousand dollars."

"But I would have lost six hundred dollars."

"True, but since you're my guest, and this is by way of a business meeting…"

She shot him a look of complete disbelief.

"…and since you're really 'working' tonight, soaking up the atmosphere of Daniz, the house would have forgiven your debt."

Emily was skeptical. "Why would they do that?"

"Because my family owns the controlling interest in the casino."

"Ah." Understanding smoothed the slight frown from her brow. "I see."

They stayed at the roulette table for several more spins of the wheel before leaving it to try a game of blackjack. For the next hour and a half, Emily sampled the games beneath the gilt dome. Lazhar strolled beside her, answering her questions about the games, showing her how to roll the dice at the craps table, and keeping her champagne flute filled. When she'd had enough of playing, they toured the other rooms on the casino's lower level. The central gambling space was huge and wings to the right and left of the domed area housed two five-star restaurants connected by a wide marbled passageway lined with exclusive designer shops. They browsed, window-shopping but not entering any of the exotic shops before they returned to the central room and climbed the sweeping staircase to look into several of the private gambling rooms on the second level.

Her curiosity satisfied, Emily paused on the wide balcony that circled the casino floor. With Lazhar leaning casually beside her, she rested her hands on the polished mahogany railing, her gaze sweeping the crowded floor below.

"It's a fascinating place," Emily commented. "The air nearly vibrates with anticipation and I can almost taste the excitement."

Below them and to their right, a young woman dressed in a white evening gown, diamonds glittering at her ears, wrists, and around her throat, shrieked with delight and jumped up and down, hugging her silver-haired companion.

"I think she won," Lazhar said dryly.

Emily laughed, her bright green eyes sparkling with amusement. "I'm sure you're right." She glanced at the scene below before she asked. "You said that your family owns the casino?"

"A controlling interest," he corrected her.

"Ah." She turned her back to the balcony and fixed her gaze on him, clearly curious. "Did you spend much time here when you were growing up?"

"A fair amount," he admitted. "My grandfather loved to gamble and he'd tell my mother that he was taking me out for ice cream, then we'd come here. He taught me to play roulette before I was six and poker before I was eight."

"Did your parents object that he was teaching you to gamble instead of buying you ice cream?"

"At first," he conceded. Lazhar never talked about his grandfather to anyone outside the family circle, but something about the genuine interest in Emily's green eyes made him want to confide in her. "My mother lost her temper when she found out but after my grandfather told her that I'd learned to do math far beyond my schoolmates, she calmed down."

Emily laughed. "Did you win often?"

"Not at first. But after a while, yes."

"What did you do with all the money?"

"Put it in the poorbox at St. Catherine's."

Her eyes widened and Lazhar could have kicked himself. He'd never told anyone else what he and his grandfather had done with their earnings. The truth had slipped out, seduced from him by the warm interest in Emily's green eyes.

"That's wonderful," she said softly. "You weren't tempted to spend it on candy and toys when you were six?"

"I was," he said ruefully. "But my grandfather wisely discussed all the possible things we could do with the money, then took me to visit the nursery school at St. Catherine's. Afterward, he told me that I could decide whether I wanted to keep the money or share it with the children at the church. Of course, I chose the church."

"That must have been a difficult choice for a six-year-old to make."

Lazhar remembered very well how he'd felt when his grandfather first asked him if he really wanted to spend his winnings on candy. A reminiscent smile curved his mouth. "At first, yes. But my grandfather was a very wise man. He didn't tell me I had to give the money to St. Catherine's. He talked about how fortunate I was to live in a palace and to be able to play cards in the casino; then we walked through Daniz, in and out of the shops, through the residential districts, both affluent and poor areas. By the time we finished, I'd learned an important lesson about the responsibilities that came with the benefits of being born into the royal family.''

"And the responsibility of being royal is what made you decide to give the money to St. Catherine's?''

"Partly. But mostly I did it because I loved my grandfather. If he thought I should give the money to St. Catherine's, that was a good enough reason for me.''

"He sounds like a wonderful man.''

"He was.'' A flashbulb went off below them and Lazhar realized that they'd been standing in full view of the throng on the floor below for too long. The paparazzi had clearly found them. He turned his back to the railing and held out his arm, elbow bent. "Are you ready to move on to the next stop on our tour of Daniz nightlife? Or do you want to chance your luck at another table here in the casino?''

"I'm ready to continue the tour.'' She took his arm and they moved down the sweeping staircase.

They said good-night to Esteban and left the casino. Lazhar's car waited on the paved forecourt, the driver holding the door open. A small crowd of photographers began snapping photos the moment they left the building.

"Just smile and wave," Lazhar advised Emily, keeping her moving forward at a smooth pace. Moments later, they were in the car, doors closed, and the limo was purring smoothly away from the brightly lit building.

"Goodness, is it always like that?" Emily asked.

"Not always. The local media has a long-standing arrangement with my family—they respect our privacy and in exchange, we have a publicist that arranges photo ops and information releases on a regular schedule."

"So photographers don't usually follow you when you're out for the evening?"

"No, but ever since the tabloids publicized my father's wish to see Jenna and I married, the international media has flooded Daniz with reporters and photographers. They're not so willing to stick to the schedule set up by the palace office." He shifted, his wrist grazing against the bulk of the roll of bills forgotten in his jacket pocket. "I nearly forgot about this." He shoved his hand in his pocket and took out the bundle of money, holding it out to her. "What do you plan to do with your winnings?'' he asked, setting the thick roll on her lap.

''I have no idea. It's a lot of money.'' She glanced at him, the streetlights flickering light and shadow over her features. ''I know.'' Her dimples flashed as she laughed. ''Let's drop it into St. Catherine's poorbox.''

Arrested, he stared at her for a moment before his mouth quirked. ''You're sure you want to do that?'' His voice held amusement. ''You could buy a lot of candy with that much money.''

''I'm sure.''

''Whatever you say.'' He leaned forward. ''Nico, stop at St. Catherine's.''

Moments later, the limo eased to the curb and Lazhar handed Emily out. He caught her hand and led her up the flight of stone steps and into the dim church. Not five minutes later, they hurried back down the steps and reentered the car.

''I wonder what the Sisters will think when they empty the box this week.''

''They'll probably think an angel visited them in answer to prayer.'' Lazhar raised their linked hands to his lips and brushed a lazy kiss against her knuckles. ''And they'd be right.''

Emily couldn't catch her breath to respond. His warm mouth barely grazed her fingers, but she felt the impact down to her toes. And the heat sim-

mering in his eyes made her heart stutter in reaction.

The car slowed and braked to a stop. She tugged
her fingers from his, glancing out the side window
to see a small sign swinging over an arched doorway, the soft rose-colored neon spelling out Pilar's.

"Where are we?"

"At a friend's club." The bodyguard pulled
open the door and Lazhar exited, turning to hand
out Emily.

Emily stepped out beside Lazhar and waited
while he spoke in Spanish with the bodyguard.
They were joined by three men from the black sedan that pulled up and parked behind the Mercedes
limousine. Emily hid an amused smile. She hoped
they weren't planning to fade into the background,
because the four tall, burly men would never be
mistaken for anything other than what they were—
men whose duty it was to guard the prince of
Daniz.

The liquid, musical Spanish conversation flowed
around her but she didn't understand a word of the
discussion. While she waited for them to finish, she
glanced with curiosity first up, then down, the cobbled avenue. The city street they stood on was narrow and winding, lined on each side with stone
buildings five-stories high, each festooned with
wrought-iron balconies dripping with trailing flowers and greenery. The sweet scent of climbing

LOIS FAYE DYER   117

roses mingled with lavender and spicy carnation to
drench the night air with perfume.

Lazhar might claim this evening was strictly
business, she thought, but for her, it was a dream
come true. Daniz seemed very exotic and foreign
to her and the sights and smells of the principality
were seducing her senses.

And then there was Lazhar himself. The handsome prince was proving to be much more than a
charming face with royal connections. If she
wasn't careful, she thought, she'd find herself falling in love with the man beneath the royal trap-
pings.

And that would be a disaster. He would soon be
marrying someone else, a woman with a pedigree
to match his lineage and the training to become the
queen of Daniz. Loving him would guarantee her
a broken heart.

The car door slammed, the sound drawing her
attention back to Lazhar just as he finished speaking with the burly bodyguards.

"Sorry to keep you waiting," he murmured. He
took her arm, his fingers warm, the calluses faintly
rough against her skin.

"Is everything all right?" She glanced over his
shoulder at the two men following close behind
them.

"Everything's fine." His hand left her arm to
rest on her waist and he moved her ahead of him

through the door held open by one of the body-guards. "They wanted to leave two men outside to watch the entrance in case the photographers followed us. I convinced them to come inside and enjoy the music and food."

A wave of sound greeted them. The unmistakable strum of twelve-string guitars accompanied the staccato rap of boot heels against bare wood floors, nearly drowning out the murmur of voices, muted laughter and click of glassware.

"Lazhar! Welcome, my friend."

Emily stepped back as a big bear of a man wrapped Lazhar in a hug and planted a kiss on each cheek.

"Joaquin," Lazhar laughed and returned the hard hug.

"I haven't seen you for at least two weeks. Where have you been?" the man demanded.

"Out of town. I've just returned, and I brought someone to meet you and to see Pilar dance." Lazhar caught Emily's hand and drew her forward. "Emily, I'd like you to meet Joaquin. He owns the club."

"I'm very pleased to meet you," she said politely. Joaquin had black eyes and a strong nose above a curved black bandido mustache that drooped over his upper lip, giving him a ferocious look. Given his size and the rest of his demeanor, she would have found him intimidating if not for Lazhar's warm endorsement.

"It's a pleasure to meet any friend of Lazhar's, especially a friend as pretty as you are." He winked at her.

"I hoped we'd be able to see Pilar dance," Lazhar said. "Is she here?"

"Yes, she is, but..." Joaquin shrugged one massive shoulder. "A new costume isn't working and she's temperamental tonight. Who knows what her performance will hold."

"Pilar only dances better when she's upset," Lazhar said with amusement. "And temperamental is Pilar's normal mood."

"*Si.*" Joaquin grinned, his teeth flashing whitely against his coal-black mustache. "My Pilar is a woman of strong emotions, not a woman of calm and serenity—which only makes the flamenco more passionate, eh?" Without waiting for a response, he gestured at a waiter. When the young man quickly approached, Joaquin issued orders in a spate of Spanish and the waiter bustled off. "Now," Joaquin continued, giving them his full attention once more, "your usual table is being prepared. If you'll come with me?"

He led them through an archway at the end of the entry hall and into a large, low-ceilinged room. They wound between crowded tables arranged in a semicircle around an open space of bare hardwood floor.

Lazhar was greeted with familiarity by more than one person as they crossed the room and each time, he acknowledged them with a smile and a greeting that included their name.

Emily wondered if Lazhar was a regular visitor at the club for his arrival didn't cause the speculation and exclamations from the crowd that she'd seen at the casino.

"Do you have time to join us for a drink?" Lazhar asked Joaquin as he seated Emily at a horseshoe-shaped booth, upholstered in burgundy leather, on the far side of the room.

"Let me check on the kitchen staff and if all is well, I'll be back to catch Pilar's performance with you," he promised, taking Emily's hand in his. He bent and kissed her fingers with an old world courtesy that was entirely natural. "It is a pleasure to have met you, Emily." He released her and grinned at Lazhar. "Emily will make a beautiful bride."

"Yes, she will."

Startled, Emily couldn't gather her wits to ask Joaquin what he meant by his parting comment until he was gone. Before she could call him back, he was intercepted by a waiter. Their brief conversation ended with the young man nodding and hurrying away. Joaquin had gone barely three steps

. more before a customer caught his attention and he paused to chat with the two couples seated at the table.

"I don't think he's going to make it to the kitchen very quickly," she commented.

"Not likely," Lazhar agreed. "He treats every customer as if they're a family friend and they love him for it."

"What did he mean by saying that I'd make a beautiful bride?" she asked Lazhar, half-turning to face him on the leather seat. He sat beside her, one arm resting along the top of the booth, his fingers within touching distance of her nape. A candle flickered in the center of their table, adding its faint glow to the dimly lit room, but still, his face seemed shadowed, his gaze enigmatic.

"I think he was stating the obvious," he said smoothly. "You're a beautiful woman. It follows that you'll make a beautiful bride when you marry." He glanced away from her at Joaquin, who was now three-quarters of the way across the room, still chatting with customers. "Joaquin is part-Spanish, part-Danizian, and he tends to assume that all young, beautiful women will marry someday."

"And you think that's all he meant?" Emily was distracted by Lazhar's matter-of-fact, almost casual observation that he thought her beautiful, but she remained uncertain about Joaquin. Still, she couldn't imagine what other meaning could be attached to the club owner's parting comment.

"What else could he have meant?" Lazhar's dark gaze returned to her, sweeping over her hair and face before lingering on her mouth. He lifted his wineglass and gestured at hers. "This is another Spanish wine that I wanted you to try."

Emily allowed herself to be diverted by the abrupt change of subject and lifted her glass to her lips. The cool, slightly tart white wine was delicious. "It's very good," she agreed, wondering how much of it she dared drink since she'd already indulged in two glasses of champagne at the casino.

The soft thrum of guitars suddenly crescendoed and the crowd burst into applause.

"Ah, this will be Pilar." Lazhar bent closer to make himself heard over the crowd noise, his lips brushing her ear. "Have you seen flamenco dancing before?"

His deep voice shivered up her spine. She told herself to ignore the sensual pull he effortlessly exerted, but it was a losing battle and she knew it. The most she could hope was that she could remain outwardly unaffected so that he didn't know what his slightest touch and the sound of his voice did to her.

"No." She shook her head. "Jane had tickets to the touring company of the Madrid Dance En-

semble's performance at the San Francisco Play-
house last summer, but I had to cancel at the last
minute. A section of the program was to be flamenco...I was very disappointed to have missed
it.''

"The Madrid Ensemble has performed here in
Daniz. I thought they were quite good," Lazhar
said. "But Pilar is a star in her own right. I think
you'll enjoy this." He looked up as the guitars
strummed faster, louder. "Here she is."

The woman who swirled onto the spotlit wooden
floor between the guitarists and audience made an
instant impact. The crowd cheered and whistles
echoed through the room as she spun slowly, heels
rapping the floor in a counterpoint to the guitars'
beat. She was tiny, with exotic features topped by
braided ebony hair pinned in a heavy, intricately
wound knot at her nape. A single, perfectly shaped
red rose nestled against her black hair, echoing the
scarlet of her classic Spanish dress. She whisked
her skirts above her knees and the ruffled under-
skirt framed shapely legs clad in sheer black stockings. Her small feet were encased in black leather
heels with a strap that accentuated the delicate
bones of her ankles. She was a visual feast, beautiful and exotic. Energy poured from her, charging
the air with electricity, crackling throughout the
room as her passion for the dance infected the audience.

She whirled and dipped, her feet stamping out the rhythm with blurred speed, her castanets clicking as the guitars increased their tempo, luring her ever faster.

Emily couldn't take her eyes off the dancer and when the music crashed to a halt and she struck a pose, the entire audience burst into spontaneous applause, including Emily.

Before she had time to catch her breath and analyze the performance, however, Pilar was joined by a man. Dressed all in black, he was much taller than the petite Pilar and he radiated the same intensity and emotion. Once again the music began and Emily quickly realized that Pilar and her partner were acting out a classic male-female courtship with their dance, advancing, retreating in a pattern that stirred her and had her breathless.

"Flamenco is all sex and emotion—primal and haunting." Lazhar murmured in her ear. Emily tore her gaze away from the pair dancing in the spotlight, her gaze meeting his. Sexual attraction pulsed between them, stealing what was left of her breath. She couldn't pull her gaze from his and the need to lean forward, to cross the short space separating them and taste his mouth, was nearly overwhelming. She was hardly aware that the dance ended, the guitars going silent. The crowd roared their approval.

"You liked it." Lazhar's voice held quiet satisfaction.

Emily licked her lips, her throat gone dry. "Yes, very much," she murmured, barely able to think. She struggled to find a safe, innocuous conversational subject. The heat in his eyes told her that he knew what she was feeling and Emily's heart raced faster, the room much too warm. "She's wonderful. Is she a local woman, someone you and Joaquin grew up with?"

"No, she's Spanish." His voice was deeper, rougher than normal. "Her agent booked her into the club about five years ago and Joaquin took one look at her and fell in love. When it was time to go, the rest of the troupe left but Pilar stayed. They were married within a few months and she's been dancing here ever since. She tours Europe for two or three months out of the year but hates to leave home and Joaquin for longer."

"She's so tiny and he's so big, they must make an interesting looking couple." Emily was grateful that Lazhar had followed her lead but despite their carefully polite conversation, tension and heightened awareness crackled between them.

Lazhar grinned, his eyes crinkling at the corners, the lines of his face softening with amusement. "He can pick her up with one hand, but trust me, Pilar may be tiny, but Joaquin has to fight for his share of influence in their family."

The guitarists began a set of mellow music. Lazhar glanced at the polished dance floor, quickly filling with couples moving to the music.

"Dance with me." He caught Emily's hand, drawing her with him out of the booth.

Chapter Five

It was a mistake. He knew it the moment she turned into his arms and lifted her hand to his shoulder. He'd been taking advantage of any excuse to touch her all evening with a guiding hand on her arm or her waist. All of the contact was socially acceptable between a man and a woman spending an evening together.

But even that small physical connection had been enough to set his blood simmering. He'd forced himself to rein in the growing urge to thread his fingers through her thick sweep of golden-brown hair, slick his tongue over the plush fullness of her lower lip and taste her.

Now only inches separated her from him but holding her loosely within the circle of his arms wasn't enough, not nearly enough. The music pulsed around them, the dance floor growing more and more crowded until another couple jostled them, bumping Emily off-stride. Lazhar caught her closer, supporting her weight against his.

"Sorry," she murmured.

"Don't be." He welcomed the excuse to wrap her tighter, her slim body resting against him, her thighs aligned with his, the soft curves of her breasts against his chest, her temple touching his jaw, her silky hair brushing his throat and chin. Having his arms around her wasn't enough but he knew that they were being observed by too many eyes, friendly though they probably were. If he gave in to the urge to kiss her in this very public place, the press would pursue them more than ever. And he didn't want Emily hounded by paparazzi.

So they stayed on the dance floor, slowly swaying to the throb of the passionate guitars, until the musicians took a break. Lazhar knew he'd reached his limit; he couldn't sit next to Emily and carry on polite conversation when all he could think about was making love to her. Reluctantly he released her, stepping back only slightly, his hand resting on her waist, and nodded briefly at the two bodyguards seated at a table on the edge of the dance floor.

The two men moved quickly and by the time Lazhar and Emily stepped out onto the sidewalk, the Mercedes was waiting for them, engine running, the back door held wide.

Lazhar couldn't bring himself to release her hand and let her move away from him. Emily didn't protest so they sat silently, pressed thigh-to-thigh, as the car purred along the winding road that climbed to the palace. He could have raised the privacy window, shutting them away from the chauffeur and guard in the front seat. But though he trusted the two men implicitly, he didn't want the faintest hint of gossip to touch Emily. He'd always been scrupulously careful about keeping his personal life private and he felt even more strongly about protecting Emily. If all went as he'd planned, she would be his wife; he wouldn't give anyone cause to question her actions.

So he held on to control by his fingertips and fought back the need to pull her into his arms.

He smoothed his thumb over the back of her hand, then the silky skin at her wrist, and felt the frantic pound of her pulse beneath his fingertips. Impatient to reach privacy, he dismissed his driver and then the guard as soon as they arrived at the palace, leaving him alone to walk Emily to her suite.

Aware that security cameras scanned the corridors at regular intervals, he opened the door to her suite and followed her inside.

The room was shadowy, dimly lit only by the faint light from a bedside lamp left burning in the adjoining room.

''Lazhar, I don't think...'' Emily began, her normally clear tones husky with emotion.

''Shh.'' He silenced her with a fingertip against her lips. ''Don't think.''

He backed her against the door panels, lifted her hands to place them around his neck, and lowered his head to cover her mouth with his.

And was instantly lost in the hot, honeyed taste of her mouth that opened willingly beneath his, the press of her body that curved so perfectly against his own, the scent of her skin and hair that stirred his senses with every breath he drew.

He was drunk on the taste, scent and feel of her. He sank his fingers deep into the heavy thickness of her hair and tilted her face up to his. She murmured incoherently, her arms tightening around his neck to hold him closer as the kiss turned hotter, the press of their bodies more urgent in the thick silence of the darkened room.

Lazhar wanted her. Emily clearly wanted him. And the bedroom was only steps away. But when he drew back, intending to obey the urging of his body, pick her up and carry her the few feet to her bed, sanity intruded.

"Damn," he muttered, resting his forehead against hers while he struggled for control.

"What?" Emily murmured, opening heavy-lidded green eyes to look up at him, confusion vying with arousal on her expressive features.

"We can't do this."

"Why?" Awareness chased away the drowsy, passionate cast of her face. Still flushed, she stiffened and pulled out of his arms. "Of course we can't." Her voice was equally stiff. "I think you should leave now, Your Highness. Thank you for a lovely evening."

Lazhar was painfully aroused but he couldn't help smiling ruefully at the contrast between the vibrant, passionate Emily he'd held a moment before and this prim, annoyed and obviously uncomfortable Emily who faced him now.

"It was my pleasure." He caught her shoulders and bent to take her mouth in a brief, possessive kiss. "Especially this." She glared at him, speechless, and he smiled, delighted with her. "I'll see you tomorrow."

She didn't answer and he stepped outside, pulling the door shut behind him. He clearly heard the sharp thud as something hit the panels. It was probably her purse, or maybe a shoe, he thought as he moved quickly down the corridor, whistling softly, his hands shoved into his pockets.

* * *

Emily woke to the sound of birds warbling and chirping outside her room, where the early-morning sunshine flooded the garden. Despite the early hour and the late night before, she rose, showered, dressed in a bright yellow sundress she found hanging in the closet, slipped her feet into matching leather sandals, and within the hour was ready to search for the breakfast room.

She stepped out into the hall, pulling the door closed behind her, and paused, trying to remember if the maid had led her to the right or the left the prior morning.

"I think we went to the right," she murmured. She set off down the thick carpet that ran down the center of the wide hallway, leaving black-veined grey marble floor visible along both sides.

She hadn't gone far when a man wearing the blue and gold uniform of a house servant entered the hall from a side passage and walked toward her.

"Miss Parks?"

"Yes."

"His Highness, King Abbar, asks that you join him for breakfast in his garden. I'm to take you to him, should you choose to accept his invitation."

Emily smiled with delight. "I would be more than happy to join the king."

The man bowed. "If you'll follow me, please. This way." He gestured down the hallway he'd just traversed and set off, Emily walking behind him.

Once again, she quickly lost her bearings as they turned into yet another hallway and then another. At last, however, they reached the familiar door where the soldiers stood guard and her guide led her through the king's spacious sitting room and out into the sunshine.

"Good morning, Emily," King Abbar's lined face lit with a smile.

"Good morning, Your Highness." Emily let the servant pull out a chair and seat her. "How lovely of you to invite me to share breakfast with you."

"And how gracious of you to accept." The king's eyes twinkled. He gestured at the waiter, who leapt into action, deftly pouring equal streams of coffee and hot milk into the Limoges china cup next to Emily's plate. "What would you like to eat this morning? My chef will make anything you want, from American pancakes to British kippers to a Danizian omelet."

"I think I'd like an omelet."

"Excellent." He waved his hand and the servant bowed and withdrew. "That is my choice as well, together with fruit and our own Danizian version of coffee, which is a bit of a cross between Turkish coffee and Italian espresso. You must taste it and tell me what you think."

Emily obediently lifted the cup to her lips and

sipped. The rich flavor of strong coffee blended with the vanilla-flavored milk, creating a smooth, succulent drink.

"Mmm." Emily gave a small hum of appreciation, her eyes closing briefly. "This is almost sinfully delicious," she told him. "I have a favorite coffee shop in San Francisco, not far from my office, and I'd love to take this recipe home with me so I can ask the owner to make it for me. Is that possible?"

"I will have my assistant write it down for you," he smiled approvingly. "I'm pleased that you like it. How are you enjoying other things about my country? Are you having a pleasant visit?"

"I'm having a wonderful time," she said promptly. "Last night we visited the casino and a club named Pilar's where we saw flamenco dancing."

"Ah, yes, I believe that Pilar's is one of my son's favorite nightspots." King Abbar's gaze was veiled and he looked away, lifting his own cup to drink. "What did you think of our casino?"

"I was fascinated." Emily leaned forward, the heady rush of excitement she'd felt when she'd won last night returning in a gust of memory. "And I actually won at roulette."

"Did you?" The king's eyebrows winged upward in surprise. "Are you often lucky at games of chance?"

"I have no idea. Last night was the first time I've ever played roulette. Lazhar explained the system his grandfather used and when I tried it, I won. A lot," she added, still faintly incredulous at the ease with which she'd gained such a large sum.

His gaze sharpened and he watched her closely over the rim of his cup. "Lazhar told you about the gambling system his grandfather used?"

"Yes." Emily lowered her voice. "He told me that his grandfather taught him to play blackjack and roulette when he was only six years old, is that true?"

The swift grin that curved the king's mouth was as mischievous as a boy's. "Yes, I'm afraid it *is* true. My father—Lazhar's grandfather—thought Lazhar should have a chance to experience life out from under the watchful eye of palace protocol. So he took my son to many places that in retrospect, perhaps he shouldn't have, and taught him things that might have been better learned when he was older."

"But Lazhar loved him very much and treasures those memories of his grandfather," Emily said with a soft smile.

"Yes, he does." The king eyed her consideringly. "Did Lazhar tell you that?"

"He told me that he gave his winnings to St.

Catherine's because his grandfather thought he should and he loved his grandfather,'' Emily said. ''I gathered from Lazhar's words and his tone that he treasured the time he spent with his grandfather.''

''Yes, we all did.'' He sighed heavily, his expression sad.

''I assume that Lazhar's grandfather is no longer with you?'' Emily asked tentatively.

''He passed away just before Lazhar's eighteenth birthday.'' King Abbar was silent for a long moment, apparently lost in memories. Then he roused himself, visibly shaking off the brief melancholy. ''What did you do with your winnings from last night? Are you thinking of visiting the Jewel Market to search for the perfect diamond or ruby later on this morning?''

Emily laughed. ''No, not at all.'' She glanced around, saw that they were completely alone as the servants had disappeared into the king's suite. ''I did what Lazhar and his grandfather did.''

He eyed her. ''And what was that?''

''I stuffed the money into an envelope and dropped it into the poorbox at St. Catherine's.''

His thick white eyebrows lifted in surprise. Then he chuckled, the deep sound of amusement startling birds from the tree in the corner of the garden. ''How much was it?''

''About ten thousand.'' Emily frowned. ''I

think. I won seven thousand at roulette, but then I lost at the dice table and won several hands of blackjack, so I can't be sure of the exact sum, but I think it must have been around ten thousand dollars.''

''That's a tidy sum,'' he commented. ''I'm sure the sisters at St. Catherine's will put it to good use.''

Their breakfast arrived and the conversation turned to more general subjects. King Abbar answered her questions about his beloved Daniz and in turn, Emily willingly shared details about her life in San Francisco. When breakfast was finished, a last cup of coffee shared, and he reluctantly left her for his doctor-ordered morning rest, she gladly agreed to return for a game of chess before dinner that evening.

The same servant who had escorted her from her bedroom suite to the king's rooms, guided her to a sun-filled morning room where the queen and Jenna were sharing morning coffee and croissants.

''Good morning, Emily,'' Caroline greeted her. ''Did you sleep well?''

''Very well, thank you.'' Emily took the chair drawn out by a house servant, murmuring her thanks as she sat.

''I understand that you've already had breakfast with Abbar this morning,'' Caroline said. ''But perhaps you'd like another cup of coffee?''

"Coffee would be lovely." Emily waited until the servant poured the mix of rich coffee and milk into her cup. "I confess, I'm hoping to take the recipe home with me."

Jenna laughed and her mother chuckled.

"We love it, too. I used to steal sips from Papa's cup when I was tiny," Jenna said. "I think I was fifteen before he gave in and agreed to let me have coffee with breakfast."

"I didn't want you drinking coffee at all before you were sixteen and I strongly suspect that your father purposely pretended not to see you stealing sips from his cup when you were a little girl." Caroline's gaze rested fondly on her daughter and they exchanged a look of warm understanding.

Emily caught an underlying current of sadness from the two women. Beneath the queen's graciousness and Jenna's impish humor there was a thread of pathos when they talked about the king. She suspected that the emotion was due to his ill health and her heart went out to them.

"What are your plans for the day, Emily?" Caroline asked.

"I need to check in with my office staff back home, and then I'm hoping to begin preliminary work on the plans for Lazhar's wedding."

"Ooh, fun." Jenna's face lit with enthusiasm. "What will you do first?"

"I'd like to look at the venue for the event—I

assume the ceremony will be held in a church in the city and the reception here at the palace?''

"Yes, that's the traditional method," Caroline confirmed. "The church is St. Catherine's and the largest ballroom would be best for the reception." A soft smile curved her mouth. "That's where Abbar and I were married." She sighed before visibly collecting herself. "The palace chef will cater the reception, which is always preceded by a sit-down luncheon for four to five hundred people."

Emily made mental notes while fervently wishing she'd brought her Palm Pilot or at least a pencil and notepad with her.

"Mother, Emily should jot this down," Jenna said firmly, holding up a hand. "Otherwise, we'll have to schedule a meeting to go over this again in your office and it's much more pleasant doing it here over coffee and croissants. Right, Emily?" She paused, looking expectantly at Emily.

"Yes, much more comfortable," Emily agreed. "If that's acceptable to you, Your Highness?"

"Please, call me Caroline. We'll be spending many hours together planning this wedding and we may as well be comfortable together. And that's an excellent idea, Jenna." She lifted a tiny silver bell from its place beside her crystal water glass and shook it. The tinkling sound was immediately followed by the appearance of a young girl wearing the palace uniform. "Ah, there you are, Sofia.

Please bring a pen and pad of paper for Miss Parks.''

Emily barely had time to say thank you to the queen before the girl was back, handing her a gold-capped fountain pen and a leather-bound notebook.

''Thank you, Sofia. Now, where were we? Ah, yes, the ceremony is held at St. Catherine's, the reception here at the palace, and there will be four to five hundred people at a sit-down luncheon. There will probably be a thousand or so invited to the reception,'' Caroline continued. ''You'll want to discuss menus and timing with our chef, of course. And the protocol of invitations, seating, etc., will need to be coordinated by the palace diplomatic office. The most difficult seating arrangements will be those for our relatives. Our family is related through a tangle of marriages and descendants to most of the royal families in Europe, all of whom will think they should have a front-row seat.'' Caroline sighed. ''And I never can keep track of who's not talking to who at any given moment.''

''Which is why you have Maria, Mother,'' Jenna said. ''That's Mother's secretary,'' she explained to Emily as she spread jam on an airy croissant. ''The woman is amazing—she never forgets a thing.''

''True,'' Caroline agreed. ''I don't know what

I'd do without her. Now,'' she said briskly. ''What else do we need to talk about before you begin?''

''How big will the wedding party be? I'm assuming that there will be bridesmaids, flower girl, ring bearer. How many bridesmaids and groomsmen?'' There was no immediate answer. Emily glanced up from her notes to find both Caroline and Jenna looking at her with arrested expressions. ''Is that a problem? The bride hasn't discussed that with you yet? If she hasn't, I can inquire when I speak with her.'' Emily was instantly reminded that she still didn't have the bride's name. ''Will she be available later today, perhaps this afternoon?'' Caroline and Jenna exchanged a swift look, but neither responded. *What's going on here?* Emily wondered, baffled by their silence.

''That, um, that may be a problem,'' Jenna said at last.

''Is she not here in Daniz?'' Emily thought a moment. ''I usually meet with the bride in person in this preliminary stage, but if she's out of the country, we can always set up a conference call to get the necessary input.''

''Unfortunately,'' Caroline said carefully, ''that won't be possible, either.''

''No?'' *This is more and more curious,* Emily thought. Where was the elusive bride?

''No.'' Jenna shook her head, opened her mouth

as if to speak, then closed it again and looked helplessly at her mother.

Emily's gaze followed Jenna's. Caroline looked from one to the other and visibly collected herself.

"You must promise, Emily, that what I am about to tell you will not go beyond this room," she said.

Startled, Emily stared at her for a silent moment before replying. "Yes, of course."

"There is no bride."

"I beg your pardon?" Surely she'd misunderstood, Emily thought.

"There is no bride," Caroline repeated. "Lazhar isn't engaged. He has no fiancée."

"But…" Emily floundered. "But he told me he wanted to hire my firm to plan his wedding."

"Yes, I know."

"So…he *doesn't* want me to plan his wedding?" Emily was beyond confused.

"No, no, he *does* want you to plan his wedding," Caroline said quickly. "But he doesn't have a bride yet."

"Yet?"

Caroline sighed and massaged her temple with her fingertips. "I'm doing a very poor job of explaining this. Since the tabloids have announced it to the world and made it common knowledge, I'm sure you're aware that it's Abbar's dearest wish to see Lazhar married. His health is delicate and he feels a need for haste. Lazhar would move mountains to give his father whatever he wants at this stage, we all would. But in this instance, I think my son is wrong.'' Caroline paused to sip from her cup, clearly fortifying herself before continuing. ''When he told me a month ago that he meant to schedule the ceremony and choose a bride sometime between then and the wedding date, I was appalled. I told him that a person can't pick a wife the same way one negotiates a business deal but he wouldn't listen to me. So—'' she spread her hands in a gesture of helpless acceptance ''—here we are. Planning the wedding of my eldest child without a bride to make decisions with us.''

Emily was speechless. Underneath her shock, joy bubbled irrepressibly. *He isn't engaged. He's not in love with another woman.*

But he will be. The knowledge that he would choose a bride sometime in the next few months deflated the exuberant bubbles.

''Well,'' she said carefully, meeting first Caroline's, then Jenna's gaze. ''Are you two willing to make decisions that the bride normally makes?''

''You mean like the color of bridesmaids dresses, how many attendants, etc.?'' Jenna asked.

''Yes, those and others.''

''Sure,'' she said airily. ''We three can pick out colors and decide on cake flavors, can't we, Mom?''

"Of course," Caroline agreed.

"Well, then." Emily drew a deep breath. "It's certainly unorthodox and I've never planned a wedding without a bride's input before, but I don't see why we can't do it." A thought occurred to her and she shot a narrow-eyed glance at the queen. "I'm assuming that if Lazhar decides on a wife at the last moment, she won't be allowed to change all the arrangements at that point?"

"Absolutely not," Caroline said firmly. "That would make the entire project impossible."

"Then it appears to be doable."

"Excellent!" Jenna clapped her hands. "This will be fun—sort of a practice session for the wedding I might have some day."

"Do you have a groom in mind?" Caroline's voice was hopeful.

"No."

"Oh."

Emily coughed to hide an amused chuckle. Caroline was the picture of a mother hoping that her daughter would wed; Jenna equally typical of a young woman refusing to be nudged. They may be queen and princess, Emily thought, but they were no different than thousands of other mothers and daughters in this age-old tug-of-war.

"What did you think of the casino?" Jenna asked, abruptly changing the subject.

"It was fabulous," Emily replied. "I loved it."

"Did you go anywhere else?" Caroline asked.

"Lazhar took me to a nightclub called Pilar's and we watched flamenco dancers. I was fascinated. I've never had the opportunity to see flamenco before but after watching the floor show, I definitely plan to find a club in San Francisco where I can see more."

The door from the hallway opened and Lazhar strolled into the room.

"Good morning, Mother." He bent and kissed Caroline's cheek, straightening to look at Emily. His gaze flicked over the bare little sundress and he smiled at her. "Good morning, Emily. Sleep well?"

"Yes, thank you." Emily refused to acknowledge the sudden race of her heart. He was wearing faded jeans this morning, with a short-sleeved T-shirt tucked into the waistband and polished black cowboy boots on his feet. Gone was the European prince. This Lazhar could have been any American male, dressed for a casual morning at home.

Except that the watch on his wrist was a Rolex and very few men of Emily's acquaintances wore faded Levi's with quite that air of elegance.

Face it, Emily, she thought. *You're hopelessly hooked on the guy.*

"I'm on my way to the stables and I thought you might want to come with me, Emily, if you're finished with breakfast."

"First she needs to call her office, Lazhar," Jenna put in. "And she has a list of other places to visit as well. Oh, and we told her," she added offhandedly. "So you don't need to worry about letting it slip out."

Lazhar eyed his sister quizzically. "Let what slip out? What is it you told her?"

"About the bride. That you don't have one."

Lazhar's dark gaze was hooded as he met Emily's. "Really. You told her."

It wasn't a question. Indeed his tone was so neutral that Emily couldn't tell if he was pleased that she knew, or that he disapproved of his mother and sister sharing that family secret.

"I've promised not to tell anyone," she said calmly. "And they've assured me that the lack of a bride to help plan the ceremony won't impact the organizing of the event, since they'll make the necessary decisions that your fiancée, if you had one, would normally make."

He raised an eyebrow, his eyes unreadable as his mouth quirked in a half smile. "Really," he murmured. "That's efficient."

Unsure what he meant and unable to tell from his expression whether he was pleased or unhappy with their arrangements, Emily was relieved when Jenna glanced at her watch and broke in.

"Drat. I was due at the stable office ten minutes ago." She pushed back her chair and stood, round-ing the table to drop a kiss on her mother's cheek. "I'll see you two there after you've made your calls, Emily."

And with a quick wave and a cheeky grin, she was gone.

"I think that's our cue to head for the media room," Lazhar said to Emily.

"Please keep the notebook and pen, Emily," Caroline said as Emily was about to remove the pages with her notes. "You'll be making lots more notes today, I'm sure."

"Thank you." Emily rose and left the room, Lazhar right beside her. Neither of them mentioned last night's kiss, and Emily decided to chalk it up to the combination of champagne and wine they'd both drank.

She refused to let him shake her composure, regardless of the fact that she was more aware of him than ever.

Chapter Six

Emily had forgotten about the time difference between Daniz and San Francisco, and when she dialed her office number, the answering machine picked up. She left a message telling Jane that she'd call back that evening, which equaled morning in California's time zone, and followed Lazhar outside.

They left the palace and took a shortcut through a lush garden, exiting through a wrought-iron gate that let them out into a wide, paved lane. Farther down the lane to their left were the stable buildings. Directly across from them stretched a paddock where horses grazed and sprinklers turned lazily under the hot sun, creating small rainbows as they watered the already lush green grass.

Lazhar crossed the lane to the paddock fence and whistled. The dozen or more horses grazing within the enclosure looked up, ears pricking with interest. On the far side of the pasture, a white mare whinnied and trotted toward them, a long-legged filly at her side.

"How beautiful," Emily murmured, so riveted by the horse that she was barely aware she spoke aloud. Head up, small ears pricked forward, her tail a banner held high, the mare's fluid gait was pure poetry. Beside her, the little white filly shadowed each movement her mother made as if attached to her by an invisible cord.

The mare slowed to a walk as she approached the fence, coming closer until she could bump her nose against Lazhar's chest. He laughed and took a lump of sugar out of his pocket, holding it on the flat of his palm. The mare daintily lipped the cube from his hand, her strong teeth crunching the little square.

"This is Sheba," Lazhar told Emily, straightening the white forelock between the horse's intelligent brown eyes before stroking his palm down her nose. "And her baby, Elizabeth."

"Elizabeth?" Surprised, Emily looked at the purebred Arabian baby. The little filly's wide-spaced dark eyes, dish face, beautiful conformation, and delicate-boned long legs made her a miniature copy of her mother.

"Jenna named her—Elizabeth was born the day after my sister watched the BBC production of *Pride and Prejudice* for the first time."

"So she's named after a Jane Austen heroine?" Emily laughed. Lazhar looked pained but resigned.

"Her long registered name includes Shalimar, which is what I'd hoped to use as her common name. But after Jenna began calling her Elizabeth, everyone else followed suit, and now she answers to that name only." He sighed and shook his head. "A royal Danizian filly answering to an English name. Where's the sense in that?"

"Oh, I don't know. I kind of like it." Emily stretched her arm over the top rail of the white wooden fence and waggled her fingers invitingly. "Come here, pretty baby. Hello, Elizabeth."

The inquisitive filly pricked her ears, clearly listening as Emily crooned. Tentatively she stretched her neck toward the fence, her nose not quite touching Emily's fingertips, and blew a gust of warm air against her palm. Then she jumped back to race off, jolting to a stop several feet away before spinning to run back to her mother. The little horse stopped on the far side of the mare and peered around her mama's chest at the humans.

Charmed, Emily laughed aloud. "She's darling."

"She's pretty cute," he agreed with a half grin.

"Will she stay here when she grows up?" Emily asked, looking around at the idyllic pastoral setting. It seemed the perfect place for a horse.

"Yes." Lazhar gave the mare one last pat and stepped back from the fence. "We're a breeding farm, so many of the fillies and colts born here are sold away from the stables, but Elizabeth won't be. Her mother belongs to me, not to the palace, and I bred her to a stallion owned by the king of Saudi Arabia. She has impeccable bloodlines and she'll live her life out here at the farm where hopefully she'll give birth to many colts and fillies as valuable as she."

"And just as cute?" Emily asked, turning to look over her shoulder for one last glimpse of the little filly. Sheba stood at the fence, watching Lazhar walk away, but Elizabeth was already caught up in other things, nosing at a leaf on the ground.

"Probably every bit as cute."

They reached the stables; the doors stood open and they turned down the wide corridor that ran from one end of the huge barn to the other. Box stalls lined both sides of the alleyway and horses shifted in the occupied stalls, coming to peer out over the top of the gates to watch Lazhar and Emily go by.

Lazhar greeted them by name, stopping to introduce Emily to the individual mares and tell her a little about them.

"Back in San Francisco, when I researched you and your family on the Internet," Emily said as they strolled on after he'd fed a mare a sugar cube from what seemed to be an inexhaustible supply. "I read an article that said the palace stables are world-famous and that your family has been breeding Arabian horses for generations."

"That's true," Lazhar confirmed as they walked out of the shaded alleyway between the stalls, redolent with the scent of hay, saddle leather and horses. The cobbled courtyard beyond was surrounded by stone buildings and the narrow alleys between them led to grassy pastures. They passed grooms leading mares, Arabians with proud small heads and dainty ears, lush tails that nearly brushed the ground behind their back heels, and glossy coats. Several of them were heavily pregnant, their bellies round with foals. "The son of the first king of Daniz married a Saudi princess and part of her dowry was a stallion and mare from her father's herd. That pair was the beginning of the Daniz Stud."

"You have quite a family history," Emily remarked as they strolled across a cobbled forecourt, through a stone archway, and reached a low building with Office printed on a small brass sign beside the heavy door.

"A great deal of tradition is tied to that history," Lazhar agreed. "But unlike my ancestors, I can waive the dowry for my wife. She doesn't need to be rich—my family has all the money it needs. I can marry where I want—and if I choose, I can wed her even if all she has in the world are the clothes on her back."

Before Emily could react to his flat statement, he pulled open the door and motioned her inside. The office, cool after the heat outside, was empty.

"Jenna?" Lazhar crossed the room and disappeared down a short hallway. In seconds he was back. "She must be out in the stables somewhere." He glanced at his watch. "We don't have time to hunt for her if we're going to visit the Jewel Market this morning."

They left the office and retraced their steps to the palace, Lazhar leaving Emily at her door. A half hour later, after freshening her makeup and collecting her purse, she sat beside him in a gleaming silver Porsche as he negotiated the curving road leading into the city.

"This is St. Catherine's." Lazhar gestured to their right as they slowed for a turn.

"It looks a bit different in the daylight," she said, gazing at the soaring arches and towers of the church. She and Lazhar had climbed the stairs and entered the quiet church after leaving the casino the night before in order to drop her winnings in the poorbox. The tower lights had glowed against the night sky and the interior had been softly lit with minimal lighting. Today, the soft rose-colored stone had a patina of age, the graceful church an elegant grande dame of buildings among her century-old neighbors. "I believe your mother said that, according to tradition, royal weddings are held at St. Catherine's?"

He nodded, glancing at her as he downshifted to climb a hill. "St. Catherine's for the wedding ceremony and the palace for the reception." The breeze ruffled his hair, his eyes concealed behind sunglasses. "Remind me to introduce you to Antoine Escobar—he's the chief of protocol for the family and can give you all the details about which wedding traditions are set in stone and what you can change if you wish."

"Perhaps I can talk to him this afternoon?"

"If we return to the palace early enough, certainly."

Emily made a mental note to remember the protocol chief's name as Lazhar swung the car to the curb and turned off the engine. "We'll leave the car here." He leaned toward her to point out her window and down the side street. "The Jewel Market is just down the street, the large building with the pillars and dome. I thought you might want to walk from here and browse in some of the shops on our way.''

"I'd love to, thank you."

Emily stepped out onto the sidewalk just as Lazhar's bodyguards, parked in a dark sedan behind them, exited the car, exchanging nods with Lazhar.

"I didn't realize the guards were following us," she commented.

"They go everywhere with us since the paparazzi invaded Daniz," Lazhar confirmed. "After the wedding, I'm sure life will settle down once again and the reporters will get bored and leave us to chase another story. In the meantime, I've doubled the guards for family members. Jenna and I can no longer move about as freely as we once did."

"Does it bother you, being the focus of so much attention?" Emily asked.

He shrugged. "No, I can't say it bothers me, exactly, but it does make life a bit more inconvenient."

They paused outside a spice shop. Narrow wooden carts edged the wall on each side of the doorway and held small bins filled with a display of spices. Emily closed her eyes, breathing deeply to draw in the heady scents of coriander, cinnamon, nutmeg, lemons and so many other intriguing flavors that she couldn't identify them all.

"Want to go inside?"

She opened her eyes to find Lazhar watching her, his face amused. "It smells heavenly." She gestured at the bright colors on the carts. "And it looks gorgeous."

They stepped over the stone doorsill and entered the small shop, Lazhar loitering at her side as Emily browsed the scented shop, fascinated. She paused to watch the shop owner scoop nutmeg into a paper cone, then twist the top closed. He repeated the action with several other spices before the woman handed over her coins, tucked her purchases into her shopping bag, already bulging with fruit, and left the store.

They followed her outside and moved on down the street, pausing to gaze into shops. Emily purchased a cut-crystal glass vase for Brenda at a china shop and a bottle of Spanish wine at a vintner's for her brother, Cade. Lazhar handed her packages to one of the bodyguards to carry and they strolled on. They reached the end of the street that led to the Jewel Market and paused, waiting for traffic on the busy main street to slow before they crossed. The small crowd waiting on the curb allowed them privacy, although they smiled and nodded, some bowing with respectful deference. Emily assumed they were native Danizians and perhaps accustomed to seeing members of the royal family on the streets.

Lazhar turned to speak to one of the bodyguards,

his attention distracted, and in that brief moment, a small child, no more than two or three years old, wiggled free of her mother's grasp and darted into the street.

Emily didn't pause to consider her actions. Without a thought for her own safety, she ran after the little girl, sweeping her up into her arms just as a car bore down on them. Horns blared and the driver slammed on his brakes, the tires squealing in protest. The edge of the car's bumper grazed her skirt as she leapt to safety on the curb and was grabbed by Lazhar, held safe in his arms.

"What the hell are you doing?" he roared, his arms tight bands around both Emily and the little girl.

Shaking from the adrenaline still coursing through her veins, Emily lifted her head to answer him but was silenced by his grim expression. Behind the dark lenses of his sunglasses, she thought she glimpsed fear in his eyes, but couldn't be sure.

The child, silent until now, whimpered. Emily looked down at her and managed a smile. "Hey, sweetie," she crooned softly. "It's all right. Don't be scared. You're fine."

The crowd around them, shocked into silence by the speed with which the life-and-death rescue had occurred, began to stir.

Emily wiggled, trying to loosen Lazhar's bruising grip. At first, he just stared at her, but then he seemed to realize that she wanted to be set free and his arms abruptly released her. But his hands settled possessively on her waist, his heavier male body a solid wall behind her.

She looked around for the child's parent just as a woman, sobbing hysterically, pushed her way through the crowd to reach them.

"Mama!" The tiny girl held out her arms and Emily let her go, surrendering the sturdy little body to her frantic mother.

She was instantly aware that her legs were wobbly, her hands trembling in the aftermath. Lazhar's hands tightened on her waist, easing her back slightly until she rested against him, his much broader bulk supporting her smaller frame.

"How can I thank you, miss?" the mother said, her daughter clutched tightly in her arms. "One moment she was next to me, the next moment she was gone. If you hadn't been so quick to run after her…" Fresh tears trembled on the young woman's eyelids, spilling over to trickle down her cheeks.

Impulsively Emily reached out to comfort the distraught mother, her hand closing with sympathy on the woman's bare forearm. "But she's safe now." She smiled warmly at the woman, clad in a clean but faded dress and the black-haired, dark-eyed little girl in a worn, too-small red jumper.

"And I bet you won't let go of your mother's hand again, will you? Streets can be very dangerous."

The little girl nodded solemnly, her gaze fixed on Emily's face, before she turned to pat her mother's cheek. "Streets are dane-ja-rus, Mama. I have to hold your hand."

"Yes, baby." The woman smiled through her tears, exchanging a look of female amusement with Emily. Her gaze moved past Emily and her eyes rounded, evidently unaware until then of the identity of Emily's companion. "Your Highness." She bowed, executing a graceful semicurtsy.

Around them, the crowd followed her example as the women curtsied, the men bowed.

Lazhar exchanged greetings with them, taking time to speak quietly to mother and child. Emily was instantly reminded of his position as the prince of Daniz and the respect and affection the residents felt for him. What she didn't realize was that those same Danizians were smiling approvingly at her, nodding knowingly at each other as she and Lazhar said goodbye and crossed the street to reach the Jewel Market.

"Are you sure you want to do this?" Lazhar asked as they entered the stone building. His hand cupped her elbow as they walked through the metal detector and then halted, waiting for the body-guards to circle the detectors, flash their badges, and be waved on by the inspectors. Lazhar drew her into the relative privacy of an alcove, his back to the entryway, sheltering her from the view of passersby.

"What? Visit the Market?"

"Yes. We can leave it till another day."

His voice was clipped, his big body tense.

"Would you like to skip our tour today and come back later?" she asked, uncertain why he was so edgy.

"Not if you feel up to touring the Market. Are you sure you wouldn't like to go back to the palace and rest?"

"Why would I need to rest?" She was having difficulty defining what his problem was, did he think the car's bumper had hit her when it had actually only grazed her skirt?

"You could have been killed back there. Don't you feel the need to recover?" His voice was carefully even, a direct contrast to the tension that gripped him.

"No. My legs were a little rubbery after it was over and we were back on the curb, safe and sound. And my hands were shaking. But I'm over that now." The muscle ticking in Lazhar's jaw didn't ease. Emily tried again. "I'm fine, Lazhar, just fine. But I'd be happy to go back to my room and rest, if you're still concerned. Would you like to return to the palace?"

"What I'd like is for you to stop jumping in front of moving cars," he ground out.

"I don't make a habit of jumping into traffic. In fact, I've never done so before." She tilted her chin and faced him, narrowing her eyes at his stormy features. "What is your problem?"

"My 'problem' is that you seem to take your safety too lightly," he said through clenched teeth.

"I do not," she said promptly. "I'm normally very cautious. Although," she admitted reluctantly, "I usually think carefully before I act and I confess I didn't think just now. When I saw the little girl running into traffic, I didn't consider what might happen. I just ran to catch her—it was purely instinct, no planning."

Lazhar's hot black gaze scorched her for a long moment. Then the tension in his big body eased, his eyes softening. "You have the instincts of a lioness with her cubs, Emily." His face solemn, he brushed the backs of his fingers down her cheek in a slow caress. "Will you protect your own children so fiercely?"

The stroke of his warm fingers against her suddenly hot cheek mesmerized Emily. What was it about him, she wondered, that made all her resolve to keep her distance fly out the window?

By the end of a very busy week, filled with tours of Daniz in which Lazhar showed her the best of his beloved country, comfortable breakfasts and luncheons with Caroline and Jenna while they went over lists for the wedding-with-no-bride, and long afternoons visiting with King Abbar, Emily felt as if she'd known the family forever. She'd long since fallen completely in love with Daniz's flower-scented nights, friendly people, narrow winding streets, and golden sandy beaches lapped by the Mediterranean.

Unfortunately she was afraid that she was equally in danger of falling head-over-heels in love with Lazhar. Each hour spent in his company made her admire him more. She knew it was unwise to risk her heart, but found it impossible to avoid him entirely. Not that she tried very hard, she thought, as she sat across a low game table from King Abbar, her elbow propped on the table, her chin resting on her palm while she contemplated her next chess move.

"Is the board that sad?"

King Abbar's mild voice interrupted her thoughts and Emily looked up to find him watching her with a half smile. "What? Sad?"

"Yes, sad—you sighed. And you're frowning rather fiercely at your rook and my knight," he pointed out, nodding at the carved jade chess pieces.

"Oh." Emily sat up straighter, folding her hands in her lap. "I'm sorry, I was thinking of something else when I should have been focused on the game.''

Abbar waved a thin hand in dismissal. ''No need to be sorry. The game will wait until this afternoon. Where is my son taking you this morning?''

''I think he mentioned shopping at the bazaar.''

''Ah.'' The king's smile widened. ''You'll enjoy that, I'm sure. Caroline loved to visit the bazaar to buy little trinkets and household goods when we first married. The palace storage rooms were filled with every conceivable thing she may have wanted, but she said we should have our own, bought just for us and our family.'' His voice lowered and he leaned forward to whisper. ''I suspect the underlying reason was that my wife simply loves to shop.''

Emily laughed. ''Many women do,'' she whispered back. ''I know I do.''

''You do what?''

Lazhar's lazy inquiry startled Emily. She hadn't heard him enter his father's sitting room. She glanced over her shoulder, her heart doing its accustomed little skip as he walked toward the table where she sat with Abbar.

''Love to shop.'' She was pleased that her voice was calm and didn't betray her increased heart rate and faster breathing. ''Your father was just telling me that the queen enjoyed shopping in the bazaar as a young bride.''

"She still enjoys the bazaar," Lazhar said dryly. "She and Jenna can spend hours picking out fresh fruit and vegetables for dinner. And even more hours if the linen maker has a new shipment of lace from Italy."

The king chuckled, his eyes twinkling as he nodded his agreement. "That's my Caroline. She barely notices fine diamonds and rubies, but mention handmade lace and she can't reach the shop quickly enough."

Emily's interest was piqued. "Will we visit the shop that carries handmade Italian lace this afternoon?"

"If you'd like."

"I'd like," she answered promptly. She moved her knight to a new square, removing one of Abbar's pawns from the board. "Can we continue our game this afternoon, Your Highness?"

"Mmm-hmm," he murmured, pondering her move and analyzing his possible answering moves. "Take her to the bazaar, Lazhar, and when you return, Emily, we'll finish our game."

"Excellent."

Lazhar held her chair and Emily rose. King Abbar leaned back in his chair, weariness in every line of his thin body but a smile of genuine pleasure on his face as he looked at the two of them standing together. "Enjoy yourselves."

They crossed the room and were on the threshold when Abbar spoke. "I'm delighted with your choice of a bride, Lazhar. You have my blessing."

Emily froze, her startled, disbelieving gaze flying to Lazhar, but he was looking at his father and she couldn't see his eyes.

"Thank you, Father."

Before Emily could speak, Lazhar's grip tightened on her arm and he hustled her through the door, past the guards and down the hallway. He threw open the first door across the hall from the suite they'd just left and urged Emily inside, releasing her to close the door and lock it behind them.

Emily spun to face him. "What did he mean by that? He approves of me as a bride? We have his blessing?"

"My father believes that you're the woman I'm marrying."

The blunt statement stunned Emily. She stared at him blankly, trying to assimilate what he'd just told her.

"How did that happen? What made him think we're getting married?"

"He likes you. You heard him, we have his blessing," he said obliquely.

"I'm the wedding planner, not the bride." She thrust her fingers through her hair in agitation. "How could this have happened?" She took three quick steps away from him and spun to stalk back. "You have to tell him. Now."

"I can't."

"Of course you can! You have to."

"I can't. He liked you the first time he met you and every day since you arrived, he's grown more attached to you and to the idea that you'll be part of his family. I don't have the heart to tell him you're not the one."

"But you'll have to tell him sooner or later," she argued, nonplussed at the situation. "He's going to notice when you say 'I do' and the woman standing beside you isn't me!"

"Yes, he would," Lazhar said grimly. "If he lives long enough to attend the wedding."

Emily was shocked into silence. "I had no idea he was…" She paused, a lump in her throat. She swallowed thickly. The lump moved lower, settling under her breastbone. In the short week she'd been in Daniz, she'd developed a genuine fondness for the king. "How long?"

"The doctors can't, or won't, give us a date. But not long." He voice was bleak.

"I'm so sorry, Lazhar." Needing to comfort him and be consoled in return, Emily stepped closer and laid her hand on his arm.

He instantly covered her fingers with his own, his warm hand trapping hers against his hair-roughened, muscled forearm. "I don't want to disappoint him, Emily. He's grown very attached to you this week and it would devastate him if he learned that you're not going to be his daughter-in-law.'' His fingers tightened over hers. ''Which is why I have to ask for your help.''

''My help? With what?''

''My father's greatest wish, perhaps his dying wish, is that I marry. I can't wait six months to find a bride. I need one now. He already loves you, Emily, and wants you as part of our family.'' Lazhar paused, then looked into her eyes. ''Marry me.''

Chapter Seven

His blunt words struck Emily speechless. She stared at him, thinking for a moment that she'd misheard him. But his face was set, his expression grim and determined; she couldn't doubt he meant what he said.

Marry me. Under different circumstances, she would have been overjoyed if he'd said those two words. But he wanted to marry for his father's sake. He didn't love her. How could she want to say "yes" and "no" all at the same time? she thought wildly.

Her usual cool composure was destroyed and her

panic must have shown on her face because his gaze softened, the hard lines of his face easing.

"I can see I've shocked you."

She pulled her fingers from beneath his, turning to pace away several steps before facing him again. "That's an understatement." She thrust her fingers through her hair, thoroughly unsettled. "It's noble of you to want to move heaven and earth to make your father happy, but marriage seems like a drastic step."

He shoved his hands into his pockets, his face inscrutable. "The marriage can be annulled, after—" He stopped speaking.

Emily's heart hurt at the unspoken acknowledgment that his father's time with the family was limited. In the short week she'd been in Daniz and observed Lazhar with his father, she'd realized that the father-son bond between them was undeniably powerful. And even though her acquaintance with the king was of short duration, she, too, felt a deep affection for him.

"How long…" She paused as her voice wavered, tears clogging her throat. "How long do the doctors think he has?"

Lazhar's answer shocked her.

Should she do this? *Could* she do this—marry a man for a few weeks in name only?

Emily had a quick mental image of King Abbar smiling at her as they played chess, heard again his words of praise and gentle pride in her when Lazhar told him about the child in the street, remembered the love on Caroline's and Jenna's faces when they spoke of him.

The slight headache she'd woke with that morning grew a little stronger and she rubbed her aching temples with her fingertips.

"Isn't there someone else that can be your pretend-bride?" She gave up trying to ease the headache. "I'm sure I read somewhere that royal families pick out fiancées for their children the day they're born. Don't you have one of those?"

"No, I don't." He shook his head, a bemused smile lifting the corner of his mouth. "Where did you read that?"

"Probably somewhere on the Internet," Emily said, refusing to be distracted.

"And even if I did have a childhood fiancée," Lazhar continued. "It wouldn't change the fact that you're the one my father wants. You're the only person that can do this, Emily."

"You're sure? You're absolutely positive that there's no alternative solution?"

"I'm sure."

"I'd have to talk to Jane about the schedule at the office." She frowned at the swift satisfaction that flashed in his eyes and was just as quickly banked. "I'm not promising that I'll do this," she warned him. "But I want to help. I've grown attached to your father in the time I've been here and if it's at all possible for me to be away from the office for a couple more weeks, I'll go along with your scheme. But I can't destroy my business in the process.''

"Understood." He nodded. "And thank you, Emily, you won't be sorry.''

She thrust her fingers through her hair again, ruffling it even more. "I hope not." She wasn't convinced, but was willing to try to work out a solution.

"Your firm won't be hurt financially," he assured her. "And it's probable that the cachet of planning a royal wedding will enhance your business portfolio, so in the long run, Creative Weddings may be a stronger company.''

"True." Emily agreed. She looked away from him, considering the possible complications her agreement to pose as his fiancée might cause. "What about the publicity factor?''

"What about it?''

"I'm assuming that the reporters will find out about our pretend engagement, whether you tell them or not. How will you explain a marriage that only lasts for a few weeks?''

"I'll deal with that when the time comes. Since that won't happen until my father is gone, I'll have bigger issues to cope with and the gossip about my short marriage probably won't seem that important."

"No. I suppose it won't." Suddenly the details of how a pseudoengagement and marriage would work didn't seem important to Emily, either. They were small indeed, compared to the loss of a man who was a beloved father, husband and ruler over a country whose residents adored him and would deeply mourn his passing. "All right," she said with sudden decision. "I'll do it."

"Excellent." The fine tension that held him dissipated, his voice filled with relief.

"We have to tell your mother and Jenna the truth."

"No." Lazhar was adamant. "My mother can't keep a secret from my father. He'll know she's hiding something and when he asks, she'll spill everything. And Jenna's the same with my mother. Neither of them can lie to each other or to my father."

"Which means that I have to lie to them." Emily narrowed her eyes at him. "I don't lie."

The corners of his mouth quirked, his eyes amused. "You never lie?"

"Not purposely." She lifted an eyebrow at his patent disbelief. "Lies create only losing situations and they can destroy lives."

"True." He eyed her consideringly for a moment. "I agree with you, Emily, but in this instance, telling my mother or Jenna is tantamount to telling my father. And if he knows our marriage isn't real, then none of this will work.''

She wasn't happy. And when she wasn't happy, her bottom lip plumped out in a very un-Emily-like—and sexy—pout. Lazhar badly wanted to haul her into his arms and kiss her senseless but he kept a tight rein on the urge. He'd been struggling to control the instinct to claim her ever since she'd agreed to their marriage and elation had roared through him.

He knew she was attracted to him. He also knew she was fighting it. She was skittish around him, holding him at arm's length with polite conversation, but when they were body to body, his mouth on hers, she melted like hot wax.

He'd crossed his fingers inside his pockets when he'd told her that their marriage could be annulled. He was gambling that before they reached that point, she'd admit that the marriage worked. It was true he wanted her to marry him because his father had quickly become attached to her, but with each day that he spent with her, he increasingly wanted her for himself.

He didn't just want her, he craved her.

And that had never happened with any other woman.

Lazhar refused to think about what that might mean beyond the fact that the sexual attraction between them was hotter, more compelling, than anything he'd ever felt before.

"There has to be a way to do this without lying to everybody," she insisted.

"Not that I can think of." He shook his head. "My father is still the king and the ruler of Daniz, despite his poor health. He has contacts and sources that even I'm unaware of—if we tell anyone that our engagement and wedding aren't real, he'll find out."

Clearly unhappy, Emily frowned and gave in. "All right," she said reluctantly. "But I still think it's wrong."

"So do I," he agreed. "But I can't come up with an alternative. We can't tell anyone, and we have to go through the traditional courtship phases, otherwise, Father will never believe us."

"Traditional courtship? What does that entail...exactly?"

Lazhar managed not to smile. Despite his casual words, she had immediately honed in on the courtship reference and she was eyeing him with suspicion. "Probably pretty much what makes up an American courtship—spending time together, meeting the parents, receiving an engagement ring, a presentation ball, instruction by the protocol officer as to the duties of a princess and future queen." He shrugged. "Just the usual stuff."

"Just the usual stuff," she repeated. "Protocol

lessons on how to act when the bride is a princess and future queen, and a presentation ball? Trust me, Lazhar, those are *not* part of an everyday, normal American courtship.''

''Perhaps not, but the rest is perfectly ordinary. Given your background as the daughter of wealthy parents and your business experience in navigating society weddings, you're uniquely prepared to cope with the palace rules that govern my family's public life.''

''I hope you're right,'' she muttered. ''Okay.'' She drew a deep breath. ''We'll tell them tonight?''

''Yes—unless you'd like to tell Jenna and Mother now. The sooner the better as far as I'm concerned, but the timing is up to you.''

Emily glanced down at herself, her lashes lowering and shielding her eyes from him. His gaze followed hers, skimming the curves beneath the simple rose-pink sundress she wore. Strappy leather sandals left her feet nearly bare, her toenails painted with a rose enamel that matched the dress.

''I'm not dressed for an important occasion— and telling your mother that I'm going to be your wife is very important.''

Lazhar thought she looked good enough to eat, but if she felt the need for a less casual outfit, he was amenable. ''Then let's go to the bazaar as we originally planned, and while we're out, we'll stop at a jeweler's and pick out a ring.''

A flash of panic moved over her face, quickly replaced by resolution. She visibly straightened and tilted her chin slightly.

''That sounds like a good plan. Perhaps we can tell your parents and Jenna at dinner tonight?''

''If that's what you'd like to do.''

''I would.''

The trip to the bazaar, followed by a visit to an exclusive jewelry store near the Jewel Market, marked the beginning of a whirlwind day for Emily. She worried all afternoon about the prospect of telling Lazhar's family that she would be his bride, but after the initial surprise, both Caroline and Jenna were elated. King Abbar was equally pleased, though he believed that they were merely formally telling him something he already knew.

Now that they knew that Emily was to be the bride, Caroline and Jenna threw themselves whole-heartedly into the preparations for the wedding. They agreed with Lazhar that the ceremony should take place as soon as possible and together, they decided to set the date for a Saturday, two weeks away.

Given the army of assistants available to the royal family, Emily thought pulling off a wedding this big in two weeks might be possible, but just barely. She'd organized several hundred weddings over the last few years, but this time, she knew she would not only have to coordinate all the details of the gala event, but she would also have to handle all of the things that only a bride could do— like standing perfectly still for an hour while the designer bridal gown was fitted.

She desperately needed Jane.

Before Lazhar left the family gathering to escort his father back to his room, Emily told him her plan to enlist Jane's help. Then she pleaded exhaustion from the eventful day and returned to her suite. She kicked off her shoes, grabbed the phone and dialed Jane's home number in San Francisco.

Jane picked up on the second ring.

"Hello?"

"Jane, thank goodness I caught you in."

"Emily? Is that you? Where are you?"

"I'm in Daniz, and yes, it's me. I think." Emily padded into the bedroom and sank onto the comfortable bed. The linens were turned back invitingly, the lemon-yellow silk sheets subtly rich against the leaf-green of the coverlet.

"You think?" Jane's voice sharpened with concern. "Is everything okay?"

"Yes and no." Emily tucked her feet under her to sit cross-legged, her apricot skirt a pool of lush color against the bed covering. "The good news is, Creative Weddings is definitely going to plan the Daniz royal family wedding…''

Jane's crow of delight interrupted her.

''…the bad news,'' Emily continued when Jane calmed. ''Is that I'm the bride.''

''*What?*''

''I know,'' Emily acknowledged, easily picturing the disbelief and confusion that must be visible on her friend's pixie face. ''It's a long story, Jane, and I'll explain everything, I promise. But first, I need to know how quickly you can get here. What's the schedule like at the office?''

''Actually it's not too bad. Once the clients knew that you were in Daniz to consult with the prince about his wedding, they were so delighted that they might be sharing *their* wedding consultant with a royal family that they've all been amazingly cooperative. Also, the staff from the Daniz Embassy has been incredible. One of the women, Trina, is a natural and Katherine Powell adores her. In fact, I think she's trying to talk her into going back to Hollywood to work as her personal assistant.''

''Really?'' Emily laughed. ''I hope Trina has a lot of patience.''

''That's what I told her. Katherine is definitely high maintenance—which of course, is probably one of the issues that you're concerned about in the office. But you can stop worrying, all is well.''

"That's a huge relief," Emily admitted. "Do you think you'll be able to clear your calendar and fly to Daniz? I can't do this without you."

"I think so." Jane's voice turned serious. "Emily, are you happy? I have to tell you, when you left here with the prince, it never occurred to me that you were the bride he was searching for."

"It never occurred to me, either," Emily assured her. "But, now I am. It's complicated, Jane, and not something I can explain over the phone. But I'll tell you everything when you get here, I promise."

Jane's sigh came clearly over the phone line. "All right, Emily, but curiosity is killing me. Be prepared to be grilled the moment I get there."

"I'll explain it all, I promise, as soon as possible. Now, tell me about the Benedict wedding, did you find the Irish lace that Mrs. Benedict wanted for the gown?"

By the time Jane rang off, after bringing Emily up-to-date on the details of her clients' plans, Emily was confident that Creative Weddings was functioning smoothly despite her absence.

She returned the portable phone to its base and realized, as a wave of weariness washed over her, that the long day had sapped her energy. She was exhausted. Within a half hour, she'd stripped off the peach-tinted silk gown and hung it away in the closet, showered, pulled on a thigh-length white chemise nightgown, and slipped into bed.

The following morning, Emily had breakfast from a tray in her room while she used her laptop to make lists for the many details of the wedding. At nine-thirty, a servant knocked on her door to deliver an invitation to join the queen for early-morning tea. It wasn't until she entered Caroline's sitting room, however, that she realized that she was the queen's only guest, neither Jenna, Lazhar, nor the king were present. The queen sat alone at the round, linen-covered table tucked into an alcove looking out on her beloved garden. Filmy draperies let the light in through the floor-to-ceiling windows but kept out the sun's glare. A delicate English bone china tea service sat in front of her and the table held only two place settings.

Uh-oh. Emily took one look at Caroline's face and nearly panicked. *She knows we lied to her.*

"Good morning, Emily." Caroline's grave expression lightened with a fleeting smile. "Won't you join me."

"Thank you." Emily sat in one of the dainty, silk-covered rose chairs, shaking out and smoothing her napkin over her lap.

"That will be all, Theresa, I'll ring if I need you."

The serving girl nodded, bowed and quit the room.

With the ease of long practice, Caroline poured tea into two fragile teacups, passing one to Emily. "Do try the almond cookies," she commented as she followed the steaming tea with a small serving plate loaded with pastries and cakes. "They're one of my favorites and the chef always includes them with my morning and afternoon tea. Although," she added wryly as she stirred honey into her cup, "I'm sure they're responsible for that last stubborn five pounds that I just can't seem to budge, no matter how much I diet."

"I think we all struggle with 'the last five pounds,'" Emily said.

"Some of us more than others." Caroline's smile faded. "I wanted to talk with you privately about the wedding, Emily."

Emily managed not to wince, but just barely.

"I know my son can be very persuasive and difficult to refuse when he wants something," Caroline continued, "but if he's pressured you, in any way, to convince you to marry quickly, you must tell me and I'll talk to him. A woman's wedding day is very important and you should have the day you've always dreamed of—you shouldn't be so rushed that your big moment is spoiled."

Emily had braced herself to hear the queen demand an explanation of the lies she and Lazhar had told her about their pretend engagement and marriage. She was so surprised by the queen's offer to intercede on her behalf, that she was at a loss for words. "I don't know what to say," she managed finally.

"Just tell me what's in your heart," Caroline said encouragingly.

Emily remained silent, frantically trying to think of a way to explain without telling further lies.

When she didn't speak, Caroline lifted her cup and sipped, eyeing Emily over the rim. "Marrying into the royal family can be an overwhelming prospect. Believe me, I had concerns before I said yes to Abbar, and they didn't all go away before the wedding, nor even immediately after," she added, returning the delicate cup to its saucer. "Let me be frank, Emily. I know my son well and I have no concerns about his desire for this marriage. However, I have the feeling that you may be having second thoughts about the wedding."

"No." Emily didn't have to lie about this—all of the reasons she'd agreed to marry Lazhar were still valid. She understood his driving need to grant what may well turn out to be his father's last wish.

"Then you do love my son?" Caroline asked gently.

She should immediately say "yes." She knew she should. Not only was it what Caroline needed to hear, but it was also the first truth in all the lies she'd been mouthing since she'd agreed to cooperate with Lazhar's plan.

But for her heart's sake, Emily knew she should say no. She should deny loving Lazhar, both to Caroline, and to the prince himself.

He's going to break my heart, she thought, acknowledging the fear that had subconsciously tormented her ever since she'd agreed to marry him.

Falling in love with a royal prince who only wanted a temporary wife was emotional suicide. How could she have let this happen, she thought wildly. Now that the date was set and they were publicly committed to the wedding, she realized that she desperately wanted a real marriage with Lazhar. And there was absolutely no hope of that ever happening.

"Emily?" Caroline's concerned voice drew Emily out of her thoughts and she realized that the queen was watching her, concern written on her patrician features.

"I'm sorry." She managed a small smile of apology. "I was distracted." Her gaze met Caroline's. "I love Lazhar more than I ever thought it was possible to love someone."

Her voice rang with conviction and her sincerity brought an instant smile of relief and delight to Caroline's face.

"Well, that answers that," she said. "And you're positive you don't feel pressured to marry sooner than you would like?"

"No, not at all." And it was true. Emily didn't

mind having the wedding quickly. The sooner begun, the sooner done, she thought. If she focused on the practical aspects of what she was doing, then perhaps she could forget that this wasn't to be a normal marriage, but a marriage in name only.

"Very well." Caroline nodded decisively. "Then it's settled. We can proceed with the arrangements." She opened a folder lying to the left of her teacup, scanning the top sheet before handing it to Emily. "This is your schedule for the day. A rather full one, I'm afraid, but we've much to accomplish if you're to be married in less than two weeks."

Emily nodded. The list divided the day into fifteen-minute increments and was booked so completely that she would have little time to spend with Lazhar, and virtually no time to be alone with him. Given the scorching kisses they'd shared, the lack of privacy between them was a good thing, Emily thought, because she wasn't at all sure she could resist him. And the more physical intimacy between them, the harder it would be to leave him when she had to go back to San Francisco alone.

But as determined as Emily was to keep distance between them, Lazhar was equally determined to have her as close as possible.

He joined Emily, Jenna and Caroline for lunch, only to have his mother whisk Emily away to a meeting with the palace staff, followed by a fitting for her wedding gown. Frustrated, Lazhar bided his time. Before dinner, he leaned against the wall outside the door to her suite, waiting.

His patience was rewarded when Emily opened the door and stepped into the hall, closing it behind her before she turned and saw him. She gasped, her hand flying to the black lace bodice of her gown, to press just over her heart. "Lazhar! You startled me."

"Sorry." He threaded his fingers through hers and tucked her arm beneath his, keeping her close as they walked down the hall. "I didn't mean to frighten you. I wanted a few moments alone with you to ask how you're coping with my family and the wedding plans."

Emily's fingers tightened on his. "Your mother asked some very pointed questions at breakfast but I think my answers satisfied her."

"What did she want to know?"

"She was concerned that rushing the marriage wouldn't give me the wedding I may have dreamed of having. She was very sweet, actually." Emily glanced sideways, her gaze meeting his for a moment before her lashes lowered and she looked away, facing forward so that he saw her profile and couldn't read her eyes. "She volunteered to talk to you and stop the wedding, if I wanted."

Lazhar tensed. "And what did you tell her?"

"I assured her you hadn't pressed me to choose an early wedding date."

"But I did, didn't I." Regret flooded him. "I was so focused on marrying you that I didn't give enough thought to what this might do to your dream of the perfect wedding." He bit off a curse, impatient with himself for having been so dense. He'd been thinking of their days together as man and wife, and that he could give her the children and home she'd told Brenda she wanted. He'd totally forgotten that the wedding itself might be Emily's first concern. He should have known better; Jenna had been planning her wedding since she was a little girl. "I'll do whatever it takes to make the ceremony as close as possible to your dream. Tell me what you want, and I'll get it for you, Emily. I didn't mean for you not to have—"

"Lazhar." She broke in. "There isn't anything about this wedding that doesn't exceed all my hopes or expectations." A smile curved her mouth, her eyes sparkling with laughter when he continued to frown at her. "It's a royal wedding, for goodness' sake. What girl doesn't dream of having a royal wedding?"

"There isn't some detail you want changed— flowers, the dress, something?" She shook her head in response but he wasn't convinced. "You're sure?"

"I'm positive."

Lazhar's muscles relaxed. "Good. What else did you and my mother discuss?"

"The details of the wedding, mostly we talked about the schedule for the next few days. It's going to be crazy."

They reached the closed door to the family dining room. Emily stopped, turning to look up at him. Her green eyes were dark with concern. "I really don't like lying to your family. I wish we could tell your mother and Jenna the truth."

"We can't. I regret it as much as you do, and I respect your wish to tell them what we're doing, but none of this will work if my father learns the truth. We can't take that chance."

She sighed heavily, the fabric of her gown tightening over the swell of her breasts. Lazhar determinedly kept his gaze on her face.

"All right," she conceded.

Unable to resist, he bent and pressed a quick kiss against her soft mouth. "It will be fine, Emily," he promised. He pulled open the door. "Have you talked to your family? Are they coming to Daniz for the wedding?"

"I called Brenda—she's very excited and says she wouldn't miss it. I couldn't reach my father but I left a message with his secretary, and I'm waiting to hear from my sister and brothers."

He nodded, silently acknowledging her comment, mentally making a note to make sure that as many of her family members as possible were present for the occasion.

"By the way," he said as he opened the door. "The family jet is picking up your friend Jane in San Francisco. She'll be here late tomorrow evening."

Her eyes widened, her fingers tightening on his. "Thank you so much." Delight mixed with relief in her voice.

"No problem. I know you want her help with the wedding details. If there's anything you need, Emily, you only have to ask."

They crossed the threshold, entering the dining room to join his family for dinner.

Emily kept reminding herself that her engagement to Lazhar was a sham and their marriage would be solely because of the king's ill health and Lazhar's love for him. Nevertheless, with each considerate, thoughtful thing Lazhar did, and with each additional hour spent in his company, she fell more deeply in love with him. Providing his jet to fly Jane to Daniz was such a sweet thing to do, she thought as she donned her pajamas later that evening.

Jane arrived late the next evening and knocked on Emily's door before eight the next morning. Still in her pajamas, Emily was so glad to see her familiar face beneath her blond curls that she could have cried.

When they were seated comfortably on Emily's bed, steaming teacups in hand and a plate of the queen's favorite almond cookies between them, Jane fixed her with a commanding stare.

"All right, tell me everything."

"Oh, Jane...where should I start..." Emily pushed her tousled hair back from her face.

"Start at the beginning," Jane said promptly.

"Very well. As you know, the original plan was to spend a week or so here in Daniz, gathering information to put together a proposal for Creative Weddings to handle Lazhar's wedding."

Jane nodded, her eyes gleaming with interest behind her wire-frame glasses.

"Somehow, the king misunderstood. Instead of seeing me as a consultant who perhaps might be hired to plan his son's wedding, he decided that I was the woman Lazhar had chosen for a bride. And before I could untangle the confusion and explain to him who I really was, Lazhar convinced me to go through with the wedding."

"Did he seduce you? Threaten you?" Jane bristled.

"No, of course not," Emily said hastily. "The media reports about the king being ill and wanting to see Lazhar married before he dies are true, Jane. He's very, very ill. He's also one of the sweetest, kindest, most wonderful men I've ever met.'' She stared into her teacup without really seeing the amber liquid. ''I'm not sure how it happened, but I've grown so attached to him in the short time I've been here that I couldn't bring myself to hurt him by telling him I wasn't marrying Lazhar.''

Jane's face was troubled, her brown eyes filled with concern. ''But Emily, how can you marry the prince just to make his father happy? What chance will your marriage have if you start out on such shaky ground?''

Emily trusted Jane completely and she badly needed to tell someone the truth. She leaned forward so her whispered words would only reach Jane's ears. ''It isn't a real marriage, Jane. His physicians have told the family the king has very little time left and after he's gone, the marriage will be annulled.''

Shocked, Jane's eyes widened. ''You're kidding?''

''No, I'm absolutely serious.''

''So, your marriage to the gorgeous prince is a complete fake? The big wedding, the title of princess—it's all only for a few days, or weeks, and then it's over?''

''Yes.''

''And when it's over, what then? Do you come back to San Francisco and go back to running Creative Weddings as if nothing happened?''

"That's the plan." *Except I doubt that my life will ever be the same again,* Emily thought.

"Wow." Jane shook her head in astonishment, visibly trying to absorb the impact of what Emily had just confided to her. "This is wild." Her eyes narrowed. "You can't let the press know," she said firmly. "They'd rip you to shreds. Heaven knows what kind of spin they'd put on your story, but it wouldn't be kind."

"I know," Emily agreed. "You're the only person, besides Lazhar and myself, who knows this isn't a real engagement. He won't even let me tell his mother and sister, because he swears they can't keep anything from his father and we don't want him to know the truth, of course."

"What are you getting out of this, Emily? I mean—" Jane shook her head, her gaze shrewd "—it's easy to see what Lazhar gets, but what about you?"

"I get exactly what I hoped to get when I came here—I'll plan a royal wedding. The cachet of that connection for Creative Weddings will be invaluable and my business will expand from the States to Europe."

"But if you're divorced shortly after you marry, you'll be notorious. The tabloids will go crazy."

"True." Emily shrugged. "But I doubt that will harm the business. In fact, the attraction of having an ex-princess as their wedding planner might pull in more clients.''

"You're probably right," Jane said dryly. "Americans love celebrities. What about your fee for all this?''

"You mean for planning the wedding?''

"Yes." Jane nodded. "And for posing as the bride. Is he doubling the usual fee for your services?''

"No. In fact, I insisted that Lazhar have his attorneys draw up a prenup agreement that dealt with all the financial issues. I'm sure the palace would have done it anyway, but I wanted to be sure it covered our particular circumstances. He assured me he would find a way to word the agreement so no one knows we plan to separate quickly.''

Jane's eyes darkened, her expression worried, a tiny frown veeing her eyebrows as her lips pursed.

"What?" Emily waited, sure that Jane had something important to say.

"Are you sure you can do this and survive with your heart in one piece, Emily?''

Emily had never managed to conceal her emotions from her best friend. She couldn't lie to her. It was so like Jane to cut to the heart of the matter. "No, I'm not sure. But I'm sure I want to do this." Jane looked unconvinced and Emily knew she couldn't explain the connection she felt to King Abbar. "I know this probably doesn't make sense to you, but I'm positive that I want to do it. I've only known the king a very short time but I felt an instant affinity with him—almost as if he were the father I always wanted.''

''And never had,'' Jane put in, her tone leaving Emily in no doubt of the dislike she felt for Walter Parks.

''No, my father isn't anyone's idea of the perfect parent,'' Emily conceded. ''But that doesn't mean I can't appreciate a man who's clearly adored by his family. If taking a few weeks of my life to play the role of princess will make him die happy, then I'm willing to do so.'' She waved a hand at the room where they sat. ''And it's not as if I'm enduring any hardships to do it, Jane. Not only is my business gaining stature, but I'm living in a palace, visiting exotic locales, meeting fascinating people. All very good stuff.''

Jane shook her head, her blond hair brushing her shoulders. ''I can't argue with any of the benefits of this arrangement you've agreed to. But, you're the last person in the world I'd expect to be involved in something like this, Emily.''

''What do you mean?''

Jane spread her hands, tea sloshing dangerously close to the rim of the delicate cup in her hand as she gestured. ''You never lie. I don't think I've even heard you utter a half-truth to anyone. Oh, sure, you're diplomatic and sometimes you don't tell the stark truth. Like the time Mrs. DiAngelo asked you if an avocado-green dress was perfect for her as mother-of-the-bride, and you managed to convince her that the pale pink evening suit was more flattering to her complexion. If you'd told her the real truth," Jane said darkly, "you would have told her that she has excruciatingly bad taste in clothes and the green dress was unspeakably ugly. Which is exactly what I wanted to tell her."

Laughter surprised Emily, lightening her mood. "Thank goodness you didn't tell her that, Jane."

"I wanted to." Jane sipped her tea and lifted an eyebrow, surprised. "Yum, this is wonderful."

"The queen has it mixed specially for her. It's delicious, isn't it?"

"Yes. I know you love tea, Emily, but it's never been my favorite. However, I could be convinced to drink this every morning. And these cookies are incredible." She took one from the plate and ate it in two small bites.

"Those are the queen's favorites, too. The palace chef makes them specially for her and since she knows I love them, she asked him to always serve them with my tea tray, just as he does for her."

Jane heaved a theatrical sigh. "Are you sure there's no way this marriage can't be permanent? Because I have to tell you, Emily, living in the palace has definite perks, not to mention the fact that Prince Lazhar is absolutely gorgeous.''

Emily smiled and shook her head. ''No, I'm afraid not. But for the moment—'' she lifted a cookie from the plate and saluted Jane with it ''—we can indulge in all the perks we want.'' She popped the dainty cookie in her mouth, chewed and swallowed. ''Or as many as we can fit in between the endless list of things to accomplish before the wedding day.''

Jane rolled her eyes, set her cup aside and dusted off her fingers. ''Where's the list? And do you really think we can pull off a royal wedding in less than two weeks? I thought you originally said that six months was going to be an extremely tight schedule.''

''Six months would have been difficult, and two weeks would be impossible if the family hadn't agreed to an abbreviated version of the traditional royal wedding.'' She slipped off the bed, walked into the sitting room to collect her notebook from the table where she'd left it late the night before, and returned to rejoin Jane. ''Here's the schedule for today,'' she handed Jane the sheet prepared by the queen's secretary.

Jane silently scanned the schedule before looking back up at Emily. ''You're booked in fifteen-minute increments, Emily.'' She glanced at her watch. "Starting in forty minutes. What can I take care of on this list for you today?"

"I thought you could take my notes and check in with the palace protocol officer—he's coordinating the church and reception invitations and seating. Then the palace florist needs some personal attention—I'm confident that they know exactly what I want, but I don't want to ignore them. It's important that everyone feels they're a vital part of the team."

"Of course." Jane glanced at her watch again. "You'd better finish getting dressed. You only have thirty-eight minutes left before your first appointment."

"Right." Emily slipped off the bed and moved quickly to the bathroom. She paused at the door to look back. "Jane, I'm *so* glad you're here to help me. I can't tell you how much I appreciate your flying in at such short notice."

"Are you kidding? I'd have been furious if you hadn't called me." Jane's face lit with a grin and she winked at Emily. "This is going to be great fun. Now get dressed."

Feeling immeasurably relieved and cheered by Jane's practical approach, Emily disappeared into the bathroom.

Chapter Eight

The wedding was spectacular.

The hot Mediterranean sun poured golden light over Lazhar and Emily as they exited the church, pausing at the top of the stone steps to wave at the crowds filling the streets around St. Catherine's. The people of Daniz cheered and tossed flowers in the air, covering the church steps with roses. They were clearly delighted with their prince's choice of a bride.

"They love you," Lazhar whispered in Emily's ear as they waved to the noisy crowd.

Emily nodded, continuing to wave and smile as

they moved down the flight of stone steps to the limousine waiting at the bottom. She was still dazed by the kiss he'd given her after they'd taken their vows. When he'd lifted her white lace veil and took her in his arms, she'd expected a brief touch of his lips on hers to satisfy tradition. No matter how brief or polite, however, she knew any kiss from Lazhar would be electric and she'd mentally braced herself to remain calm and composed. But the kiss began with such tenderness that it shook her preconceived notions and ended with a carnality that left her feeling he'd physically and publicly claimed her as his.

For a groom that supposedly wanted a temporary marriage, Lazhar was acting amazingly like a future lover.

Emily didn't know how she felt about that. And she had little time to consider it as the car whisked them back to the palace for the first of the festivities, a late-afternoon brunch for five hundred of their closest friends and important dignitaries. The brunch was followed by the wedding reception that took up the evening.

It was nearly midnight before Emily and Lazhar could bid their guests farewell and escape to his private residence in the southern wing of the palace.

Emily was unfamiliar with this section, but she easily recognized the uniforms of the guards who were posted at the entrance to the wing. The reception gaiety continued unabated far below them on the first floor, on the other side of the palace, but here all was quiet, the hallway empty except for the two of them and the guards at the entrance behind them.

The hall was decorated much as the other areas of the palace and had a lovely Persian carpet runner, its colors glowing beneath the light from the gold-and-crystal sconces installed at regular intervals on the walls. Oil paintings hung between the sconces, the stunning seascapes and florals interspersed with family portraits.

"This carpet feels so good after standing on marble floors all day," she remarked, relishing the cushioning beneath her aching feet. She was tempted to stop, lift her skirt and slip off the white satin, narrow-heeled pumps. She loved the way the shoes looked, but they were killing her feet.

Lazhar paused outside a door, turned the knob and pushed it open. Then without warning, he bent and swung Emily into his arms.

She gasped and clutched at his shoulders. "What are you doing?"

"Carrying my bride over the threshold. I understand it's an American custom." He smiled down at her, turning sideways to maneuver the long train of her white lace wedding gown through the door.

He nudged the door closed with his heel before striding across the room.

Emily gained a quick impression of a sitting room that equaled the beauty of the other rooms she'd seen in the palace and then they were in the bedroom. Lazhar halted, lowering her to the bed where the voluminous skirt of her gown pooled around her, the satin and lace startlingly white against the deep blue of the silk spread.

He caught the hem of her skirt and pulled it above her knees. Emily's heart stuttered but before she could speak, he slipped off her shoes and tossed them over his shoulder onto the floor. Then he swung her legs sideways so he could sit beside her on the edge of the bed, rested her aching feet on his hard thighs, and rubbed her instep with his thumbs.

"Ohhhhh," she groaned. This was certainly not what she'd expected when he lifted her dress, but it was sheer heaven after the long, endless day spent standing in reception lines.

"Feel good?" He lifted an eyebrow, his dark gaze assessing her face, a smile curving his mouth.

"Wonderful." Emily closed her eyes as he worked out a knot in the muscles and eased the stressed tendons. "If you ever need a second career, you could always be a masseuse," she said with a soft moan.

"I'll keep that in mind," he said with amusement.

"I thought the wedding went well, didn't you?" she asked absently.

"Very."

"I didn't realize that there would be so many Americans there, except for my family of course."

"We do a lot of business with American companies," he explained. "And quite a few of the Americans at the brunch were friends of mine from Harvard. We've kept in touch over the years."

Intrigued, Emily opened her eyes and looked at him. The room was shadowy but the lamp on the bedside table threw a pool of light over the bed where they sat. Lazhar's hair gleamed with blue-black highlights, his lashes lowered over dark eyes as he focused on her foot. She wore skin-toned, thigh-high stockings and her foot in the pale hose seemed small and very feminine enclosed in his tanned hands, the other resting on the black tuxedo slacks covering his thigh.

He lifted his lashes and his gaze met hers. Emily was instantly reminded that they were alone together in his bedroom, this was their wedding night, and the kiss he'd given her at the church had been far from platonic.

Emily wasn't a virgin, but her experience was limited to the man she'd been engaged to after college. Their physical relationship had been pleasant, but not earthshaking. Their engagement had ended badly when she learned that his interest in her was generated by his burning desire to advance his career in her father's company. Disillusioned, she'd thrown herself into building Creative Weddings and hadn't taken time to pursue a connection with another man since.

Still, she'd experienced the mechanics of sex and understood what the heat in Lazhar's eyes meant.

"I didn't know you went to Harvard," she commented, struggling to keep her tone light. "Tell me about it."

The slight lift of the corners of his mouth told her that he recognized her ploy, but still, he answered her. "I attended public school here in Daniz as a child but after graduating at sixteen, I wanted to go farther afield. I convinced my father to send me to the States for college and he picked Harvard."

"He picked Harvard?" Emily was diverted despite herself by his choice of words. "Don't you mean Harvard accepted your application? Or does a prince automatically have his choice of any school?"

"I suspect most college-level schools would seriously consider a prince," he admitted with a shrug. "But in my case, I had the necessary grades to be offered admittance at several schools, and my father picked Harvard.''

"Did you *want* to go to Harvard?"

"Yes." He smiled at her. "I chose Harvard, but the king had to approve the choice."

"I see. So it was a royal-protocol-thing?"

"Yes. Although I don't think it's uncommon for parents to give final approval for their children's college choice."

"You're probably right. And you were sixteen when you entered Harvard? In the States, college freshman are normally eighteen years old—did you feel out of place with your classmates being two years older than you?"

"No, it didn't bother me."

"Somehow, I can't picture you living in a dorm room and riding a bike to class," she mused, narrowing her eyes in thought.

"I didn't ride a bike to class, but I did live in a dorm room," he said.

"Did you enjoy the whole college experience—being away from home and family, all on your own?"

"I wasn't exactly on my own...my bodyguards had the room next door."

Emily stared at him in shock. "You're kidding?"

"No, I'm not."

"It never occurred to me that you would need

guards at school." She shook her head. "Especially not in the States."

"Hmm," he murmured. While they'd been talking, his fingers had left her toes and instep and move upward to her ankle. Now they moved higher, finding the tired muscles in the back of her calf and kneading.

"*Ohhh,* that's…" Indescribable, she thought. Her eyes drifted closed with sheer pleasure and she leaned back on her elbows.

He moved to her other foot, her ankle, then her calf. Emily stopped talking, lulled by the warm stroke of his palms on her skin and the firm press of hard fingers as they worked the tired muscles and eased away the aches.

Unfortunately for Emily, having his hands on her ankles and calves led to thoughts of having them on other parts of her body. Her heartbeat pounded faster, harder, surging in a rhythm directly connected to the stroke of his hands against her skin.

"Hey." His deep voice was as warm as the last caress of his palms against her calf when he released her and stood. "Don't go to sleep—you won't be comfortable in that dress."

She was relieved that he'd assumed her eyes were closed because she was tired. She didn't want him to know that his hands on her had aroused her to the point where she doubted she would be able to fall asleep at all.

He took her hands and drew her to her feet, his palms cupping her shoulders to turn her away from him. She caught her breath as he freed the button at her nape, then moved to the next one. There were thirty-two buttons from her nape to just below her waist. She knew the exact number because the seamstress had teased her about how much her husband would enjoy unbuttoning them. At the time, her only concern had been how she would manage to get out of the dress by herself, since she didn't anticipate Lazhar helping her. Now, she didn't know how she'd survive having him slip loose those thirty-two buttons.

Breathe, she told herself, determined to get through this without revealing how his touch affected her.

But with each button he freed, the back of his fingers brushed her bare skin beneath the dress. Wearing a bra hadn't been an option since it would have spoiled the line of the bodice, so the designer had incorporated a foundation garment into the gown itself.

Emily knew the moment Lazhar realized that she wasn't wearing anything under the bodice for his fingers stilled. The tip of his forefinger traced the line of her spine from her nape to just below her shoulder blades.

''You're not wearing anything under this?'' His voice was an octave lower than normal, husky with arousal.

''Not under the bodice.'' She could only manage the barest of information. The sound of his voice weakened her knees, already seriously threatened by the slow brush of that fingertip down her spine. She didn't breathe again until he moved to the next button.

He reached the fastening at her waist and moved lower to undo the final button. Then he slipped his hands beneath the open edges of the gown and stroked upward, widening the gap between the edges of the gown from below her waist to her nape. The loosened bodice sagged and Emily caught the pearl-edged lace and satin neckline, holding it against her breasts with both hands.

''Lazhar,'' she said, struggling for control as he bent his head, his mouth hot, damp against the sensitive skin at her nape. Her lashes drifted lower as he nipped her, instantly soothing the tiny sting with his tongue. ''I...we shouldn't do this.''

''Why not?'' he murmured, his hands closing over the narrow sleeves of her gown and tugging the bodice lower.

''Because making love isn't part of our plan.''

''Making love to you has always been part of my plan, Emily. I've wanted you since the first moment I saw you.''

His blunt statement shocked her. She twisted in his arms, looking over her shoulder. The hard planes of his face were taut with arousal, desire streaking dusky color over his cheekbones.

"But you said the marriage would be annulled. We never planned for this to be a real marriage—sleeping together will only complicate things."

"It doesn't need to be complicated. I want you. You want me. That's about as simple as it gets between a man and a woman." His arms slipped around her waist and he pressed her against him. "You touch me and I burn."

His arms encircled her, her naked back tight against the white linen shirt covering his chest. Emily felt the heat that poured off him, sending her own temperature higher, and the slam of his heartbeat that echoed the frantic race of her own.

His hand stroked her throat, moving upward to cup her face as he turned her in his arms. "We're married, Emily. And this marriage can be as real as we decide to make it."

"But when our few weeks together are over, what then?" Emily's palms rested on his white silk shirt. His heart pounded beneath her hands and she curled her fingers, pushing against his chest.

He let her shift away from him, but didn't release her, their bodies still touching from waist to thigh while the fingers of one hand still cupped her cheek.

She searched his face. "I'm sure the sex would be wildly satisfying, Lazhar, but I don't want an affair. And that's what we'd have."

"No." His thumb grazed her bottom lip. "Not an affair. We're good together, Emily. We make a good match. And we'd have beautiful children," he added, his hand dropping to smooth over her flat midriff.

Emily caught her breath. "Not fair." Her voice was husky with emotion. "You know I don't plan to have children."

"I also know you'll make a wonderful mother, Emily." His voice roughened, deepening. "Stay, Emily, share my bed."

"Beyond tomorrow?" Her voice sounded drugged, her body throbbing with the need to give in.

"Forever, if you'll stay." His eyes were heavy-lidded with passion, his fingers smoothing compulsively over the bare skin of her back where her dress gaped open. His hand slipped beneath hers, tugging the edge of her neckline from her grip and easing it downward.

Emily stiffened, struggling to hold back the wave of pleasure that washed over her. "We agreed to marry for only a few weeks. That's not forever," she argued. But her words lacked conviction, her protest at odds with her body's need to give in.

The bodice slipped to her waist, kept from falling farther by the tight press of their hips, leaving her bare from the waist to the crown of her head. His gaze left hers, black lashes lowering as he looked down—and his big body shuddered.

His fingers tightened on the soft skin of her back and midriff, his body straining against hers, held in check by the force of his will.

"If you're going to say no, do it now." His voice was guttural. "You've got about two seconds before it'll be too late."

And in that instant Emily knew she was going to take the biggest gamble of all.

"Yes." She slipped her arms around his neck, her breasts lifting against the warm linen of his shirt. "I want you, Lazhar."

"Thank God," he muttered. One big hand cradled her head and he bent, taking her mouth with a kiss that seared her. Then his mouth left hers and closed without preamble over the swollen, sensitive tip of her breast.

Emily moaned. Lazhar's mouth left her breast and took hers.

The white wedding dress pooled around her feet when he lifted her and swung her into his arms. Focused on the shuddering pleasure of his mouth on hers, Emily was barely aware of him carrying her to the bed. The silk spread felt cool beneath her bare back and thighs when he laid her down, lifting himself away from her to strip the brief white lace bikini panties down her legs. He tossed them over his shoulder, his eyes hot and intent on her body as he stood to shrug off his own clothes.

Burning with need, Emily watched impatiently while he shed his jacket and shirt, then unbuckled his belt and unzipped his slacks. He shoved the slacks and silk boxers down his legs in one swift movement and knelt on the bed. Emily shivered. His eyes were predatory, his broad, muscled body heated and aroused, totally focused on her. For one brief moment she felt threatened by the power inherent in his much bigger body, but then he slid his arm under her and lifted her, cradling her upper body against him while his mouth took hers, their legs tangling as he pressed against her from mouth to toes. His weight bore her back on the bed and she wrapped her arms and legs around him, binding him closer.

"Please," she murmured when his mouth left hers to take her breast once more. She twisted frantically when he stroked a hand over her hip and rocked against her. "Please…"

He growled something unintelligible and surged against her, demanding entrance.

Emily stiffened, struggling to accept him.

"Relax, honey." His voice was gravelly, taut with restraint, his muscles trembling with the effort needed to give her time to adjust.

"I'm trying." She stiffened, pinned beneath his weight, breathless, her hands clutching his biceps. "You're too big."

His hand brushed between them, finding her and stroking in small, seductive circles.

"Ohhh." Emily forgot to try to relax, totally focused now on the incredible pleasure of his touch. Lazhar flexed his hips and she cried out as he surged inside, sending her over the edge in a blinding climax. He followed her in a swift, passionate drive that left them both sated and exhausted.

She lost track of how many times they made love. Sometime during the hours before dawn, he carried her into the shower and then back to bed, where he tucked her bare body against his and she fell asleep, exhausted.

Morning sunshine filtered through the light draperies covering the tall windows and reached their bed, waking Emily. Her lashes lifted and she lay perfectly still, adjusting to the fact that she wasn't alone. Lazhar's arm was a warm, possessive weight at her waist. Her body was curved, spoonlike, against him with his powerful, hair-roughened thighs against the back of hers and her bottom tucked into the cradle of his hips. He was still asleep, she thought, reassured by the slow, gentle rise of his chest against her back and shoulder blades as he breathed.

His forearm, deeply tanned and lightly dusted with fine black hair, lay under hers. She covered the back of his hand with hers, struck by the marked difference between his much larger hand and strong, square-tipped fingers with their neatly trimmed nails and her own much smaller hand, the slender fingers tipped with pink-enameled nails. The bones of her narrow wrist seemed even more delicate next to the sturdy width of his.

She'd never thought of herself as a small woman, but Lazhar was a big man, his bones thicker than hers, his body heavily muscled, his legs longer, the reach of his arms greater. Yet despite the passionate abandon of the night before, he'd unfailingly harnessed that strength to give them both only pleasure.

What she'd shared with Lazhar wasn't the lukewarm emotion her ex-fiancé had elicited. In fact, she thought, bemused, there wasn't anything about Lazhar that was remotely like any other man she'd ever known.

"Good morning." The deep voice was raspy with sleep.

Emily had been so absorbed in her thoughts she hadn't noticed the change in the tenor of his breathing. She looked over her shoulder. His dark hair was tousled, his jaw shadowed with black beard. His gaze was heavy-lidded, growing more so as his hand left her waist and cupped her breast.

"Good morning." Her voice was throaty as well, but not from sleepiness. The caressing movements of his fingers against her breast were stealing her breath, making her bones melt like hot wax.

"Come here." He tugged her onto her back, slipped his arms under her and rolled until she lay on top of him.

Emily shivered with the abrupt sensual stroke of her body against his. Sprawled along his broad, hot length, her hips pressed to his, she was well aware of his growing arousal.

The abrupt rap of knuckles against the outer sitting-room door broke the sensual tension that bound them. Startled, Emily's eyes widened and she instinctively shifted to move away. His arms tightened, refusing to let her leave him.

"Ignore it. Whoever it is will go away. We're on our honeymoon." He lifted his head and caught her mouth with his, luring her deeper into a kiss that made her forget the sound. He wrapped his arms around her and rolled once more, reversing their positions so her soft, bare body was pinned under the harder angles of his.

But the knocking didn't stop.

"What the hell..." His voice exasperated, Lazhar reluctantly lifted away from her, bending back down to press one more hard kiss against her faintly swollen lips. "Don't move." He rolled off the bed and stalked naked across the room, grabbed his black slacks from the floor where he'd tossed them the night before, stepped into them and zipped them as he left the bedroom.

Emily lay sprawled where he left her, a faintly bemused smile curving her mouth. She shifted, stretching, and realized that she ached in places she'd never noticed before.

Her husband was an amazing lover. She knew now why she hadn't missed the physical side of their relationship when she'd split with her ex-fiancé. He hadn't touched her, not really, not in any of the ways that Lazhar had. Lazhar had stripped away all her defenses, refusing to let her hold anything back from him and the result was that she felt linked to him, branded somehow.

Mated, she thought, realizing that's what had happened between them during the long night.

The murmur of voices ceased, the outer door to the sitting room closed, and she sat up, tucking the sheet under her arms and over her breasts, to look expectantly at the bedroom door, waiting for Lazhar to appear.

When he did, he carried a breakfast tray, loaded with covered dishes, a carafe of orange juice, and another carafe that Emily hoped held coffee.

"My father had the chef send up a tray," Lazhar said with a grin. "Evidently he thought you didn't eat enough last night at the reception and since it's nearly lunchtime, decided to feed us."

"How sweet of him," Emily exclaimed, touched by her new father-in-law's thoughtfulness. "I didn't realize it until now, but I'm starving."

Lazhar set the heavy tray down atop the rumpled sheets and plumped the pillows, tucking them behind her and nearer the center of the bed. "Slide over and lean back."

Emily moved to the middle of the bed where she sat cross-legged, the plump pillows cushioning her bare back against the carved headboard, the silk sheet tucked around her.

Lazhar picked up the tray and moved it to the middle of the bed, joining her with the food between them.

He lifted the covers from two plates. "Omelets and crisp bacon." Lazhar handed one of the plates to Emily. "I'm sure this American breakfast is in honor of you, Emily—the chef and his staff want to make you feel at home."

"It worked." Emily smiled at him, setting the warm plate on her lap so she could pour coffee into two delicate Wedgwood cups. "And if they've sent us Daniz salsa for the eggs, then it's a perfect breakfast."

"Salsa?" Lazhar lifted the lids from several little pots, uncovering jam, marmalade and honey, before he found Emily's spicy red sauce. "Here we are."

They ate in companionable silence. Plates

empty, Lazhar refilled their coffee cups, handing a cup and saucer to Emily. "What would you like to do today? We can drive inland and sightsee, play tourist, if you like."

"That might be fun, I'd love to see more of—"

The phone rang, interrupting her. Lazhar leaned across her to catch up the receiver of the phone sitting on the nightstand.

"Hello?"

Emily felt his body tense and he shot her a quick glance.

"Hold on." He handed the receiver to Emily. "It's a business call. I'll take it in the other room. Will you hang up the receiver for me after I pick up in there?"

"Of course."

His gaze held hers for a moment. Then he caught the back of her head in one hand and held her still for a kiss.

"I'll be right back."

She nodded, bemused and breathless from the sudden heat that always bloomed when he touched her. *Maybe we should cancel the trip into the countryside and just stay in our room all day.*

"You can hang up now, Emily." Lazhar called from the other room.

His voice startled her and she realized she'd been sitting motionless, smiling at the door where he'd disappeared, totally distracted by thoughts of him.

"All right," she responded. She stretched to reach the phone but the breakfast tray tipped precariously. She caught it, sliding it toward the end of the bed, then twisted to return the phone.

"...she went through with the wedding. I thought we'd take care of signing the contracts today."

Emily paused, frowning at the receiver, still in her hand. That voice was unmistakable: it was her father. Why was Walter Parks calling Lazhar? Without giving a thought to the fact that she was eavesdropping, something she would never ordinarily do, she lifted the phone to her ear.

"I signed the documents yesterday...they'll be delivered to your office by courier sometime tomorrow," Lazhar said.

"Excellent." Walter's satisfaction came clearly over the line. "You won't be sorry, Your Highness. We'll both make a great deal of money from this enterprise. And I'm sure my daughter will make you a good wife. All in all, the best kind of merger, with both of us getting what we want."

"If you ever tell her, the deal is canceled." Lazhar's voice was cold, lethal.

"No, no, of course I won't," Walter said hastily. "Emily isn't likely to approve of my offering her to you as part of a gem deal, despite the fact that you needed a wife and she always dreamed of being a princess."

Emily's heart stopped, pain shafting through her. Her father had offered her to Lazhar as part of one of his high-stakes deals? And Lazhar had accepted?

"Just so you understand that this subject is never to be mentioned. Not to anyone."

"I understand."

And he's lying. He knows how I feel about telling lies.

Her hand trembling, Emily carefully eased the receiver onto the phone base. Outraged and heartsick, she sat perfectly still, her dreams of a future with Lazhar lying shattered in pieces around her.

Betrayal was an ugly word. And that's what Lazhar had done to her, she thought. Nausea shook her and she swallowed thickly, refusing to give in to the devastating heartbreak.

The unexpected sound of someone knocking once again on the sitting-room door startled her and she jumped, rattling the cups in their saucers on the tray. She heard the outer door opening, then Lazhar's deep tones alternated with another male voice before the door clicked closed.

She braced herself, trying to prepare for the confrontation that she knew must happen immediately. Staring at the doorway, she clasped her hands tightly together, waiting for Lazhar to appear.

When he did, his expression was so somber that she knew instantly something was very wrong, something not connected to the phone call from her father.

"What is it?"

"Father—he's had another heart attack."

"Oh, no." Emily clutched the sheet tighter over her breasts, fear for the king searing her. "Is he…?"

"He's alive. But his doctor doesn't know how much damage has been done. They're taking him by ambulance to the hospital."

He pulled open the closet door, disappearing inside and Emily slipped out of bed, quickly donning her silk robe. She joined him, gathering underwear from a drawer and snatching a pair of white slacks and coordinating white-and-blue knit top from their hangers. She raced into the bathroom, performing her usual morning routine in record-breaking time. When she returned to the bedroom moments later, she found Lazhar dressed in jeans and a long-sleeved white shirt, sitting on the edge of the bed to pull on socks and boots. While he used the bathroom, she slipped into sandals and collected her purse from the closet.

When he left the bathroom, unshaven, his hair damp, she was ready and they left the suite, moving quickly down the hallway. Lazhar's chauffeur had the car waiting, engine purring, and a guard opened the rear passenger door the moment they exited the palace.

The drive to the hospital was nearly silent. Despite the shock of the overheard conversation, Emily didn't object when Lazhar threaded their fingers together, resting their clasped hands on his thigh. She knew a confrontation between them was inevitable, but it would have to wait. For now, they were joined by their mutual worry over the king's health.

Fortunately the press apparently hadn't yet learned of the king's medical emergency, for there was no crowd of reporters and photographers waiting outside the hospital. Nevertheless, their driver took them around the back to a little-used entrance that assured them privacy.

Escorted by his bodyguards, Lazhar and Emily rode the elevator to the fourth floor. Here, royal guards stood sentry at intervals along the halls, the entire floor cordoned off. They moved quickly, their footsteps loud in the nearly empty hallway.

"Your mother and sister are in here, Your Highness." A guard held open the door to a private waiting room.

They stepped inside, the door closing quietly behind them.

Caroline, standing near the window, looked over her shoulder and saw them. Her face crumpled, tears welling in her eyes. "Lazhar."

"Mother." Lazhar's long strides erased the distance between them and he folded her close.

Emily held back her own tears as Jenna joined them and Lazhar hugged her as well, murmuring comfortingly to the two women. Emily looked away, struggling to hold back the flood of emotion that threatened to destroy her composure. A small kitchenette unit took up one corner of the waiting room and she crossed to the short counter, occupying herself with pouring coffee into two of the foam cups stacked next to the machine.

"Emily?"

She glanced up to see Lazhar gesturing her near and carrying the two steaming cups, she joined the trio. Lazhar took the cup she handed him, sipping without comment while she exchanged hugs with Caroline and Jenna. Both women reflected the strain, their faces tearstained.

"Have you talked to the doctors?" Emily asked.

"Just briefly," Caroline said. "They told us they had to run tests and would be back to tell us the results as soon as they were available."

"But Dr. Schaefer was certain that Father had a heart attack at the palace?" Lazhar asked.

"Yes. Abbar didn't feel well last night but we thought it was indigestion and perhaps he'd overexerted himself at the wedding festivities. He stayed in bed this morning, resting, and he was sleeping when I left to deal with morning mail and some other things that I couldn't postpone.'' Caroline's voice faltered. ''It wasn't an hour later when Maria came in to tell me Dr. Schaefer was with your father. I ran to his room and arrived just as the doctor was calling for the palace ambulance to transfer him to the hospital.''

''Maria came to my room and told me right after she saw Mom,'' Jenna put in. ''I sent Ari to tell you and Emily, then ran straight to Papa's room, but they were just wheeling him out on a gurney. We rode here in the ambulance with him.'' Her voice trembled and she pressed her fingertips to her lips, her eyes filling with tears once again.

''Shh,'' Caroline murmured, slipping an arm around Jenna's shoulders. ''Your father has the best doctors available in Europe. He's going to make it through this.'' Her last sentence was a fierce, whispered promise.

''Your Highness?''

All four of them turned toward the doorway and the man dressed in surgical scrubs who entered. Each face held varying degrees of hope and dread.

''Dr. Schaefer.'' Lazhar held out his hand and the doctor shook it briefly as he joined their group. ''How is my father?''

''He's holding his own,'' Dr. Schaefer said gravely. ''The good news is that this latest heart attack didn't damage the heart muscle. But he has blockage in two arteries that we have to deal with immediately.''

Oh, no. Emily caught her breath. *Does this mean open-heart surgery? Is he strong enough to survive that?* The memory of the king's thin hand, resting on the game pieces as they chatted between chess moves, and how frail his body seemed, filled her with dread.

Beside her, Caroline's indrawn breath was a sharp, audible gasp and Jenna clasped her mother's hand.

''We've known about the blockages for some time and the potential need for surgery, but were waiting for the king to grow stronger. We no longer have time to wait. We have to deal with them now, rather than later. However,'' he continued, his gaze meeting Lazhar's and then Caroline's, ''we have an option for treatment.''

''What is it?'' Lazhar's voice was calm, but the empty foam cup slowly crumpled in his grip.

''Instead of performing open-heart surgery, which the king may or may not survive, we can do a coronary balloon angioplasty. It's a minimally invasive procedure that will clear the blockages. Then we'll install stents in the artery to support the weakened area and prevent the blockage from recurring.''

''What do you mean by minimally invasive?'' Caroline asked, her voice strained.

"We don't have to make an incision in the chest wall," the doctor explained. "We place a catheter into the femoral artery, then insert a balloon to clear the blockage before we put in a stent."

"A stent?" Caroline asked. "What is that?"

"It's a latticed, metal scaffold, very tiny, that's placed within the coronary artery where the blockage was to keep the vessel open."

"My father talked to me a month or so ago about this procedure," Lazhar said. "And he said he'd decided not to go through with it."

"Yes, that's true," Dr. Schaeffer agreed. "But he didn't want to choose any of the possible surgical or procedural options such as angioplasty at the time. He opted to try dietary changes and alternative medicine first."

"But those options didn't work." Jenna's comment wasn't a question.

"No, they did not," Dr. Schaeffer concurred, his voice somber. "And now it's imperative that we take measures to correct the problem and a coronary balloon angioplasty is the least invasive option open to us. He was lucky this time. As far as we can tell, there was no damage to the heart. But if we don't deal with the artery blockages, there's no guarantee that he'll be this lucky the next time."

"He'll have another heart attack?" Caroline asked, her voice tense.

"Yes."

Lazhar's dark gaze met Emily's before moving on to Caroline and Jenna. Emily caught the subtle, slight nod that first Caroline, then, more reluctantly, Jenna, gave him.

"Very well." Lazhar nodded abruptly at the doctor. "How quickly can you do it?"

"The staff is prepping the operating room now."

Chapter Nine

Time inched slowly past as they waited for Dr. Schaeffer to return with a report on the procedure. A half hour into their vigil, a hospital official knocked on the door to tell them that the press had gathered in front of the hospital and Lazhar left to speak with them. Emily looked out the window, watching the surge of reporters as Lazhar stepped out of the building, four floors below.

Behind her, Jenna flicked on the television set and found a news channel. The live feed showed Lazhar nearly surrounded by the crowd of reporters and photographers, two uniformed guards at his back. His face was impassive, his voice calm as he gave a brief update on the king's condition before he was barraged by questions from the reporters.

"How does he do that?" Emily murmured, watching Lazhar respond to a reporter while several others clamored to be heard.

"He's had lots of practice," Jenna said, her gaze on the television screen. "After Lazhar came home from university in the States, Papa slowly turned more and more of his duties over to him."

Emily nodded in acknowledgment of Jenna's comment. "He seems so calm, so in control."

"He's been that way ever since the kidnapping."

Startled, Emily's gaze left the screen and fastened on Jenna. "Kidnapping? What kidnapping?"

"He didn't tell you?"

Emily shook her head.

"Lazhar was kidnapped while he was at Harvard. I think it must have happened during his second year there because he was seventeen at the time. The people that took him were radicals who wanted to rid Daniz of the monarchy. They also wanted a ton of money," Jenna added. "They held Lazhar for five days before a combination of Daniz and American security forces got him back."

Anger surged through Emily, her hands clenching into fists. "Did they harm him?"

"He had a few bruises, but no serious injuries.

It changed Lazhar, though. He seemed older after that—more serious, and that's when he took up martial arts and switched the focus of his classes to defense and military training.'' Jenna turned to Caroline, who was pacing between the bank of windows and the open door, where she paused to search the hallway before returning to the windows. ''Don't you think Lazhar changed after the kidnapping, Mother?'' Caroline continued to stare out the window and didn't respond. ''Mother?''

Caroline jerked, looking around. ''Yes?''

''I asked if you agreed that Lazhar changed after the kidnapping when he was at Harvard.''

''Yes.'' The queen pushed her hair off her forehead, distracted. ''Yes, he seemed to go from being a teenager to a man overnight.'' She frowned, her gaze focusing on Emily. ''Horrible business. He didn't tell you about it?''

''No.'' Emily shook her head.

''He probably hasn't had time,'' Jenna commented. ''What with your whirlwind courtship and now this...'' She trailed off, waving her hand to indicate the hospital room.

''Yes, that's probably it,'' Emily agreed, knowing it was more likely Lazhar hadn't told her about this traumatic event in his life because theirs was a marriage arranged for convenience, not for sharing their lives and confiding the details of the youthful experiences that had formed them. After all, she hadn't shared the private moments of her teenage years with him, either, she thought. And it was unlikely she ever would, she reflected bleakly, for as soon as she knew the king was on the mend, she would be returning to San Francisco to resume her life. Her real life. Not the fairy tale dream of marrying a prince that for one unforgettable night, she'd believed had become reality.

On the television screen before her, she saw the press briefing breakup, Lazhar reentering the hospital's wide glass doors with the two guards.

Moments later, they heard the sound of the elevator, then footfalls in the hallway, and Lazhar appeared in the doorway. His gaze swept the room, finding Emily.

"Any news?"

"Not yet." She turned away, busying herself with pouring water into the coffeemaker and measuring coffee into the basket.

He crossed the room and slipped his arms around her waist. "Are you all right?"

His voice was a low-pitched murmur, his breath feathering across her cheek, shivering her nerves.

"Yes. I'm fine," she managed to say. "Or as fine as any of us can be at the moment."

His lips brushed her throat just below her ear and Emily closed her eyes, the moment bittersweet. Then his mother called his name and his arms tightened briefly before he released her. Emily tried to breathe past the pain lodged in her chest, just over her heart, and forced her hands to finish the task of switching on the coffeepot, brushing the few spilled grounds from the counter and dropping them into the trash basket next to the cabinet.

She managed to avoid having any meaningful conversations with Lazhar as they waited. Confined as they were to the waiting room with Caroline and Jenna and sometimes members of the palace staff, it was surprisingly easy to do. Everyone was worried and distracted by the threat to the king's health.

At last, Dr. Schaeffer joined them, his green scrubs wrinkled, his face weary but smiling. "The procedure was a success," he told them.

Caroline dropped her face into her hands and sobbed. Jenna threw her arms around her mother, tears rolling down her cheeks. Emily felt her own cheeks grow damp and brushed away tears with her fingertips. Lazhar slipped his arm around her shoulders and hugged her close, tucking her face against the warm column of his throat, his grim face lit with relief.

"What happens now?" he asked. "How long will he be hospitalized?"

"At least three days and probably longer. I want to be very sure that he's completely stable before he goes home and I'd like to see him gain a few pounds."

"So would I," Caroline said, her sense of humor resurfacing through her tears.

The doctor smiled at her and Jenna gave a watery chuckle.

Lazhar reached out to shake the doctor's hand and Emily used the opportunity to slip out of his arms.

"Can we see him?" Caroline asked.

"Yes, just as soon as he's out of recovery and in his room. I'll ask the nurse to let you know the moment they've settled him in," the doctor assured her. "The staff will need some time to get everything set up, monitors attached, etc. and make him comfortable."

"Thank you, Doctor."

"Just doing my job. I'm glad I had good news to tell you. If you have further questions, don't hesitate to ask for me at anytime. I'll be staying here at the hospital until the king goes home so the staff can always reach me."

He left them, his rubber-soled shoes squeaking slightly on the waxed tile floors as his tall lanky body disappeared through the door.

The six days following the king's heart attack passed swiftly. Between the long hours Emily and Lazhar spent at Abbar's bedside at the hospital and the additional duties Lazhar assumed for his father, Emily managed to avoid being alone with him almost completely. He came to bed long after she did and the few times that she was awake, she pretended to be asleep. She didn't resist when he slipped his arms around her and eased her against him, a part of her cherishing those few moments when she could allow herself to be close to him.

She knew their time was limited, however, for she'd decided to confront Lazhar and tell him she'd overhead his conversation with her father and knew they'd used her as a bargaining chip. She would tell Lazhar and return to San Francisco as soon as the king was home from the hospital and out of medical danger.

A phone call from Brenda reminding her that the date of her father's gem smuggling trial was near only increased her determination to leave Daniz.

She went with the family to the hospital on the day the king was to be released, a part of the group as the king waved to the crowds of adoring citizens. But as soon as they reached the palace and King Abbar was settled into his rooms, the family occupied with the pleasure of having him with them once again, she gave him a last hug and kiss and slipped away to the suite she shared with Lazhar.

She was packing, her bag open on the bed, when Lazhar entered the suite. He reached the bedroom door and halted abruptly.

"What are you doing?"

She glanced at him, then back at the soft silk robe in her hands, continuing to fold it. "I'm leaving this evening, flying home to San Francisco." She carefully laid the robe in the suitcase and looked at him. "I know the real reason you married me, Lazhar. I overheard you talking to my father the morning King Abbar had the heart attack."

He looked as if she'd slapped him. "Emily." He started toward her. "You were never meant to know."

"I understand." She held up her hand and took a step back her voice shaking with pent-up anger. "Please. Don't come any closer. I'd like to end this without a big scene."

His eyebrows winged upward in surprise before veeing down in a scowl. "Well, that's not likely to happen. And you *don't* understand."

"Yes. I do," she said evenly, determined not to lose her temper. "Your conversation with my father was very clear. He offered me to you as a bride in return for concessions in a gem deal. You agreed. Oh," she added. "You also told him never to tell me."

"Because I didn't want you hurt. I knew if you ever found out about the deal Walter thought he made with me, you'd never believe that I didn't marry you because of it."

"You were right," she said coolly. "I don't."

He cursed and dragged a hand through his hair. "Dammit, Emily, you've got to let me explain."

"No, I don't." Despite her best efforts to control her anger and hurt, her voice rose. "No amount of explaining will erase the fact that you purposely married me to get a better deal from my father. It's outrageous."

"I agree. It would be. If it were true, but it's not."

"Stop. Just stop!" Emily felt her temper slip beyond her rigidly held control. "I agreed to marry you because of your father. Now that he's past the crisis, the need for this sham of a marriage is over. I'm leaving." She grabbed a handful of lingerie from atop the bedspread and threw it into the suitcase. "How I could have been so stupid as to fall in love with a man who has a business machine for a heart is more than I can understand. You're just like my father," she fumed, glaring at him.

Lazhar's eyes narrowed, shock quickly replaced by triumph. "You love me."

"I do *not* love you." Annoyed that he'd managed to ignore all her comments except the one she wished she'd left unsaid, her voice rose another level, but she was beyond caring if she could be heard outside the room. "I hate you. Didn't you listen to anything I said? You're just like my father. I want the annulment you promised and I want it now. The sooner the better."

"We can't have the marriage annulled," he said reasonably. "We consummated our vows, remember?"

"All right, then divorce me." Emily planted her hands on her hips and glared at him. She was so angry she could nearly feel steam coming out of her ears and he appeared totally unaffected. In fact, he looked amused, his arms crossed over his chest, his body relaxed, the corners of his mouth quirked in a half smile. When he didn't answer, she grabbed the last item from the bed, the black Vera Wang evening gown, and tossed it on top of the stack of clothes. Then she slammed the lid closed, zipping it with quick, angry movements.

She swung it off the bed but before she could move, Lazhar intercepted her.

"Honey, please. Put the bag down and listen to me."

She tried to step around him, but he shifted, blocking her.

Irritated, she stopped, staring at him, impatiently tapping her foot.

"I didn't marry you because of a business deal."

She lifted an eyebrow in disbelief, but remained silent.

"It's true that I was looking for a bride because of my father's health and his wish to see me married. It's also true that Walter sent me your picture along with a suggestion that I consider you as a wife as part of the deal we were working on.'' Despite the withering glance she gave him, he kept talking. ''But what Walter didn't know is that I took one look at the photo of you and ordered the plane readied to fly to San Francisco.''

Her eyebrows shot up in disbelief.

''It's true.'' He laid his hand on the blue linen shirt, just over his heart. ''I swear. Why else do you think I moved heaven and earth to get you to come back to Daniz with me?''

''Because my father asked you to and you wanted his signature on a contract.'' She shot back without hesitation.

''Emily, Walter's the one who was anxious to close the deal. Not me. I was having second thoughts about doing business with him when he sent your picture. He needed me far more than I needed him.''

''So you're saying that you *won't* make money from the contract with my father?'' Her voice was loaded with skepticism.

''Oh, I'll make money,'' he conceded. ''But I would have passed on the proposal if it hadn't been for you. The Parks business is solid, but your father is in serious trouble and were it not for meeting you, I wouldn't have linked Daniz's reputation with him.''

For a moment, Emily wavered. He seemed sincere, his voice filled with conviction. Then she remembered his cold voice as he told her father that he must never tell her about their deal, and her resolution firmed. "All of that is immaterial. I want an annulment, and if we can't get one, then a divorce."

"Even if you divorce me, Emily, I won't give you up."

"If we're divorced, you'll have to."

"No, I won't. If it takes a year of courting you, I won't give you up. I'll camp outside your door in San Francisco, send you flowers every hour, show up at your office every day—"

"That sounds suspiciously like stalking," she interrupted.

"It isn't stalking when the woman loves you. Then it's called courting."

Emily threw her hands up. "For heaven's sake, Lazhar. Why are you being so stubborn? You *don't* love me. I just happened to be available when you needed a wife and I slotted nicely into place between a gem deal and keeping your father happy."

Lazhar winced. "It sounds pretty bad when you put it so bluntly."

"Can you deny that's the reason you brought me to Daniz?" she demanded, her eyes narrowing.

"No," he admitted. "But I can certainly deny that's the reason I asked you to marry me." A muscle flexed in his jaw, all amusement erased from his features, his previously relaxed stance suddenly tense. "I know now that I fell in love with you the day I met you, Emily. Anything else became irrelevant after I'd spent less than two days with you." His forefinger lifted to brush gently against a spot near her mouth before stroking down her throat. "I love your sense of humor and the way your dimples flash when you really laugh. I love the way you genuinely care about the people around you. I love your bravery, though you damn near scared me to death when you jumped in front of the car to grab that little girl." His voice deepened, roughening. "I love the way you turn to fire in my arms when we make love. In fact—" his fingers left her throat and lifted to gently tuck a strand of hair behind her ear "—I love everything about you."

"Lazhar, I don't think..." Emily's voice trembled. She badly wanted to believe him, but she was torn.

He stopped her words by touching his fingertips to her lips. "I love you, Emily, and I want to spend the rest of my life with you. I want babies and family Christmases and everything else that goes with being married to you. Please don't throw away all we can have because I've been an idiot."

Emily could no longer deny the sincerity that was written on his features and rang in his voice.

Tears welled, spilling over to trickle down her cheeks.

"Hey," he murmured, brushing the dampness from her cheeks with his fingers. "I didn't mean to make you cry. If you can't believe me and still feel you have to go home, I swear I'll let you go. But don't ask me not to follow you. I can't let you go without trying to make you love me again."

"I haven't stopped loving you." Emily's fingers covered his, cradling them against her cheek. "But when I knew that I was part of a business deal, I couldn't believe you meant it when you told me that our marriage could be real."

"It can," he said, his deep voice husky with emotion. "If we want it to be. Do you want it, Emily? Do you want me?"

She did, she thought, the surge of love she felt for this man burning away the anger, hurt feelings, and sadness that had tormented her for the last six days.

"Yes," she whispered. "I do."

"Thank God." He bent his head, brushing open-mouthed kisses over her forehead and cheeks. Her lashes drifted closed and his lips were butterfly-light against her eyelids. Then his mouth found hers and the cherishing, reverent kisses turned hot.

Her arms locked around his neck, her hands spearing into the thick silk of his hair. He tugged her blouse loose from her waistband, his hand slipping beneath to cup her breast over the thin lace of her bra. Emily moaned and lifted heavy lashes to look up at him when his mouth left hers.

"We've been married for six days and spent only one night making love," he muttered as he stripped her blouse away and ripped open the zipper on her skirt. He shoved it down over her hips and it pooled around her feet. "I must be eligible for sainthood."

Emily smiled at him. There was something very appealing about a frustrated male tearing a woman's clothes off. Especially when the male was Lazhar.

"I know exactly how you feel," she murmured, her fingers busily unbuttoning his shirt. She reached the button just above the waistband of his jeans and tugged. When the shirt didn't easily pull free, she abandoned it and unbuckled his belt.

His arms wrapped around her while he unhooked her bra, Lazhar froze when she eased down the zipper of his slacks and slid her hands beneath the opening to wrap around him. Totally absorbed, her fingers testing the hot silk over steel length of him, Emily slowly became aware of the tension that held him motionless.

She glanced up. His eyes were closed, his face tortured with pleasure. He dropped his forehead to rest against hers and his chest rose and fell, faster and faster as he breathed deeper, visibly reaching for control.

"That's enough." His voice was guttural, strained, and he stripped the loosened bra down her arms and dropped it. His hands closed over hers, his body surging briefly against her palms before he gently removed them from his skin. "One more minute and I'd have lost it," he told her, picking her up to lay her on the bed. He stripped off the rest of his clothes and joined her, nudging her thighs apart and crawling between them. "And I don't want to do that until I'm inside you."

His mouth covered hers at the same time she felt the blunt tip of his arousal nudging for entrance. Then he slid home, joining them irrevocably; they both shuddered with relief at the surge of hot passion that ripped through them.

Two weeks later, Lazhar handed Emily out of a long black limousine in front of an upscale seafood restaurant on San Francisco's Fisherman's Wharf. Beyond the Wharf, the scenic Bay was a wide expanse of gray water, capped with the occasional white curl of foam atop waves. The breeze that blew in off the sea was tangy with salt and held the brisk chill of mid-October, teasing their hair and nipping at their faces.

Lazhar pressed a warm kiss into Emily's palm before tucking her hand through the crook of his arm, his hand covering hers against the light wool of his coat sleeve. "Are you sure you feel up to going to a party tonight?"

She smiled up at him. "Absolutely. I'm looking forward to seeing my family and a party given by Cade and Sara is a perfect way to introduce you to the Parks family members who couldn't make it to Daniz for our wedding."

"I suppose so." Lazhar looked unconvinced. "But if you get tired, tell me and I'll take you back to the hotel immediately."

Emily leaned closer to whisper in his ear. "You just want to get me alone in our hotel room."

Lazhar laughed, a deep chuckle that warmed her. "You're right. If I had my way, I'd lock the doors, order room service and keep you there for the next week." He nodded his thanks to the doorman who pulled open the heavy glass door to the trendy restaurant.

She squeezed his arm in sympathy as they crossed the threshold. "I know exactly how you feel," she confided. "But humor me tonight, okay?"

"Whatever you want, sweetheart." He dropped a light kiss on the tip of her nose. The easy, loving gesture warmed Emily.

"Check your coats, sir?"

Lazhar and Emily stopped just inside the lobby, its warmth welcome after the chilly October evening outside. "Yes, thank you." He waited for Emily to unbutton her ankle-length, light wool coat, then slipped it off her shoulders and handed it to the uniformed coat-check girl. Beneath the red coat, Emily wore a scarlet cocktail dress, the sleek little bodice held up by narrow shoulder straps, the skirt a sassy swathe of silk and lace. Below the skirt, her long, shapely legs ended in dainty feet and strappy red sandals.

Lazhar shrugged out of his topcoat, handed it to the girl, took the claim ticket she gave him, and turned back to Emily. His gaze flicked over her from the gleaming fall of shiny gold-brown hair to the tips of her toes and his dark eyes heated, gleaming with approval.

"You were wearing a red suit when I met you," he murmured as he took her arm and started toward the private banquet rooms. "I don't know how I managed to keep my hands off you that day and I have no idea how I'm going to accomplish it tonight."

"You won't have to wait all night, just until we get back to the hotel," she said, teasing.

He groaned in mock pain and she laughed. "Oh, look." She pointed at a sign on the wall behind him. The nautical letters read Poseidon Patio, and a sign pointed down the hallway before them. "I think that's where we're supposed to go."

Lazhar and Emily made their way down the hall-

way. The walls were ornately patterned with shiny
shells and conches that reflected the sea theme in
the outer lobby. The doors to the patio banquet
room stood open, the sound of laughter and voices
reaching them easily. They paused on the threshold, hands linked, searching the crowd for Cade
and Sara.

"Emily!" Brenda greeted them with delight,
leaving a small group of chatting guests to bustle
forward and enfold Emily in a warm hug.

Emily laughed and returned the hug with enthusiasm.

Brenda released her and stepped back, holding
Emily's hands in hers as she shrewdly assessed
her. "You look absolutely wonderful, hon," she
said, bestowing a brilliant smile on Lazhar.
"You've clearly made my girl very happy, Your
Highness. Bless you."

Lazhar grinned at the diminutive Brenda, his
gaze moving possessively over Emily at his side.
"Thank you."

Brenda's gaze sharpened, a tiny, inquisitive
frown pulling her eyebrows into a vee over her
nose. "There's something about you...you're almost glowing. Is there any chance..." Her eyes
widened at Emily's smile and her gaze flew to Lazhar. "Are you? Can you be...?"

Emily glanced questioningly at Lazhar, who
nodded.

"You're the first person outside the royal family to know, Brenda." She leaned closer to whisper in Brenda's ear. "I'm pregnant."

Brenda beamed. "Oh, Emily, my dear child. I'm so happy. So very happy for you." She squeezed Emily's hands tightly, tears glistening in her eyes behind the lenses of her glasses.

"Thank you, Brenda." Emily glanced at her husband, her eyes twinkling. "Just the day before I met you, Lazhar, Brenda warned me to pay attention so I didn't fail to recognize my 'Prince Charming' when he finally appeared."

"Did she?" Lazhar said lazily, smiling at the gray-haired woman his wife adored. "Then I have to thank you, Brenda, for giving my Emily such sound advice."

Brenda chuckled and slipped her arm through Emily's. "Let's find Cade and Sara and tell them the good news."

"Is my father here?" Emily asked, scanning the crowd as they wound their way across the room.

"No. Cade told me they invited Walter, but I haven't seen him yet."

"Jessica!" Emily halted their progress to throw her arms around her sister, interrupting her conversation with a fiftyish, black haired man, graying at the temples. Blond and curvy, Jessica shared Emily's dimples, a legacy from their mother.

"Emily!" Jessica left her conversation in mid-sentence to greet her sister. "How are you? I'm so glad you made it tonight." Smiling, she glanced at Lazhar. "Thanks for bringing her, Lazhar. I admit I was a little worried when you took her so far away, but now that I know you'll fly her back to visit us, I'm not so concerned."

"Emily can return to visit anytime she wants, in fact," Lazhar commented as he met Emily's eyes. "She'll be in San Francisco at least quarterly every year to check in with her manager at Creative Weddings."

"Is Jane taking over the San Francisco branch?" Jessica inquired.

"Yes, and she's very excited about it," Emily replied. "We'll work very closely, of course, which will be easy to do since Lazhar has the most amazing telecommunications facility. And she'll also be involved in the smaller European branch that I'm planning in Daniz."

"Wonderful."

Jessica would have said more, but just then, Cade called to Emily. She looked over her shoulder to see her brother, his arm slung around Sara's shoulders, beckoning to her.

"I have to go. I'll talk to you later," Emily promised.

"Okay." Jessica watched Emily, Lazhar and Brenda move off through the crowd, a small smile curving her lips.

"Both you and your sister have your mother's dimples."

"Yes." Jessica glanced behind her at Derek Moss. "I'm sorry, I should have introduced you. That was very rude of me."

He shrugged. "Not at all, you were excited to see each other." He nodded across the room where Emily, Lazhar and Brenda had joined Cade and Sara. "Does Emily keep in touch with your mother?"

"I don't know." Jessica's smile disappeared. "We never talk about her."

"That's too bad," Derek said gently. "Perhaps those of us who once knew and loved your mother should have tried harder to keep in touch. I think I'll write her a letter this very evening, renew old ties."

"That's a lovely idea." Jessica's smile returned. "I've been corresponding with her for some time and plan to fly to Switzerland soon to visit her in person. My father would be furious if he ever found out, but this is something I have to do."

Neither Jessica nor Derek were aware that they were being observed. Private Investigator Sam Fields, hired by Walter Parks to follow Jessica, leaned against the wall across the room, holding an untouched glass of whiskey.

If Jessica could have foreseen the impact that Sam would have on her life in the coming weeks, she might have paid more attention to the odd fore-boding that shivered up her spine. Instead she merely hugged herself, wondering at the sudden chill before it eased and she forgot about the in-cident, caught up in the excitement as Cade lifted his voice above the crowd noise.

"Attention, attention everyone."

The group quieted, turning expectantly.

"We have more great news tonight. Emily and Lazhar just told me they're expecting a little prince or princess in about eight months."

The room burst into cheers, applause, and shouts of congratulations. Emily flushed, laughing at some of the racier comments. Lazhar, his arm around her waist, smiled down at her and bent to press a kiss against her temple.

Cade glanced at his watch. "It's getting late. Dinner should be ready soon. Is everyone here?"

"I think so." Sara's gaze moved over the crowd, trying to count guests. "Hmm. We may still be short one or two people."

"I think I'll visit the ladies' room before we sit down to dinner," Emily said to Sara.

"It's just off the hallway outside the main door to the banquet room," Sara explained.

"I'll be right back," Emily murmured to La-zhar, who was discussing the Jewel Market with Cade. He nodded; Emily could feel his gaze following her as she made her way through the crowded room and out into the hall.

An hour later, after dessert and coffee, Lazhar and Emily joined the other guests on the dance floor.

Emily snuggled into her husband's arms, her fingers threaded into the thick hair at his nape, her body nestled against his.

"Um," she sighed happily. "I had a lovely time tonight, didn't you?"

"Yes, and now that I'm finally getting to hold you, it's even better," he said dryly. He tipped his head back to look down at her, his gaze searching her face. "How are you doing? Not too tired?"

"No, not at all. I feel wonderful. Oh, that reminds me!" She smiled, dimples flashing. "You'll never guess what happened when I was in the ladies' room before dinner. My brother Rowans' wife, Louanne, told me she's pregnant. And Sara confided that Linda Mailer, my father's accountant, is also pregnant. I swear, the baby-fairy must be waving her wand over the Parks family." She chuckled. "Brenda will be over the moon with excitement. We're going from having only Cade's little girl to three more babies in the family."

Lazhar's gaze heated and his arms tightened. He whirled her smoothly through the half-open balcony doors and out into the cool night air. He stopped in the shelter of the overhang that blocked the Pacific breeze, backing Emily up against a support column.

"I'm eternally grateful to whatever fairy or angel waved her magic wand to bring you into my life, Emily. You and our baby," he pressed his palm to her still-flat midriff, his big hand warm and possessive on her belly. Then he took her mouth in a hot kiss that melted her bones and stole her breath.

Brenda was right, Emily thought, dazed by the force of emotion that shook her. Despite her once-cynical attitude toward love, she'd found her very own prince.

*   *   *   *   *

Watch for the fifth book in the exciting
Special Edition continuity
THE PARKS EMPIRE
THE MARRIAGE ACT
by Elissa Ambrose
Coming in November 2004
Available wherever Silhouette Books are
sold!

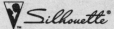

SPECIAL EDITION™

Coming in November to
Silhouette Special Edition
The fifth book in the exciting continuity

THE PARKS EMPIRE

DARK SECRETS. OLD LIES. NEW LOVES.

THE MARRIAGE ACT

(Silhouette Special Edition #1646)

by

Elissa Ambrose

Plain-Jane accountant Linda Mailer had never done
anything shocking in her life—until she had a one-night
stand with a sexy detective and found herself pregnant!
Then she discovered that her anonymous Romeo was
none other than Tyler Carlton, the man spearheading the
investigation of her beleaguered boss, Walter Parks. Tyler
wanted to give his child a real family, and convinced
Linda to marry him. Their passion sparked in close
quarters, but Linda was wary of Tyler's motives and afraid
of losing her heart. Was he using her to get to Walter—or
had they found the true love they'd both longed for?

Available at your favorite retail outlet.

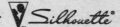

SPECIAL EDITION™

A sweeping new family saga

THE PARKS EMPIRE

Dark secrets. Old lies. New loves.

Twenty-five years ago, Walter Parks got away with murder...or so he thought. But now his children have discovered the truth, and they will do anything to clear the family name—even if it means falling for the enemy!

Don't miss these books from six favorite authors:

ROMANCING THE ENEMY
by Laurie Paige
(Silhouette Special Edition #1621, on sale July 2004)

DIAMONDS AND DECEPTIONS
by Marie Ferrarella
(Silhouette Special Edition #1627, on sale August 2004)

THE RICH MAN'S SON by Judy Duarte
(Silhouette Special Edition #1634, on sale September 2004)

THE PRINCE'S BRIDE by Lois Faye Dyer
(Silhouette Special Edition #1640, on sale October 2004)

THE MARRIAGE ACT by Elissa Ambrose
(Silhouette Special Edition #1646, on sale November 2004)

THE HOMECOMING by Gina Wilkins
(Silhouette Special Edition #1652, on sale December 2004)

Available at your favorite retail outlet.

If you enjoyed what you just read,
then we've got an offer you can't resist!

Take 2 bestselling
love stories FREE!

Plus get a FREE surprise gift!

Clip this page and mail it to Silhouette Reader Service™

IN U.S.A.	IN CANADA
3010 Walden Ave.	P.O. Box 609
P.O. Box 1867	Fort Erie, Ontario
Buffalo, N.Y. 14240-1867	L2A 5X3

YES! Please send me 2 free Silhouette Special Edition® novels and my free surprise gift. After receiving them, if I don't wish to receive anymore, I can return the shipping statement marked cancel. If I don't cancel, I will receive 6 brand-new novels every month, before they're available in stores! In the U.S.A., bill me at the bargain price of $4.24 plus 25¢ shipping and handling per book and applicable sales tax, if any*. In Canada, bill me at the bargain price of $4.99 plus 25¢ shipping and handling per book and applicable taxes**. That's the complete price and a savings of at least 10% off the cover prices—what a great deal! I understand that accepting the 2 free books and gift places me under no obligation ever to buy any books. I can always return a shipment and cancel at any time. Even if I never buy another book from Silhouette, the 2 free books and gift are mine to keep forever.

235 SDN DZ9D
335 SDN DZ9E

Name	(PLEASE PRINT)	
Address	Apt.#	
City	State/Prov.	Zip/Postal Code

Not valid to current Silhouette Special Edition® subscribers.

Want to try two free books from another series?
Call 1-800-873-8635 or visit www.morefreebooks.com.

* Terms and prices subject to change without notice. Sales tax applicable in N.Y.
** Canadian residents will be charged applicable provincial taxes and GST.
   All orders subject to approval. Offer limited to one per household.
   ® are registered trademarks owned and used by the trademark owner and or its licensee.

SPED04R   ©2004 Harlequin Enterprises Limited

SILHOUETTE

SPECIAL EDITION™

presents

bestselling author

Susan Mallery's

next installment of

DESERT ROGUES

Watch how passions flare under the hot desert sun for these rogue sheiks!

THE SHEIK & THE PRINCESS BRIDE

(SSE #1647, available November 2004)

Flight instructor Billie Van Horn's sexy good looks and charming personality blew Prince Jefri away from the moment he met her. Their mutual love burned hot, but when the Prince was suddenly presented with an arranged marriage, Jefri found himself unable to love the woman he had or have the woman he loved. Could Jefri successfully trade tradition for true love?

Available at your favorite retail outlet.

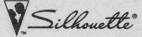

E WK

COMING NEXT MONTH

#1645 CARRERA'S BRIDE—Diana Palmer
Long, Tall Texans

Jacobsville sweetheart Delia Mason was swept up in a tidal wave of trouble while on a tropical island holiday getaway. Luckily for this vulnerable small-town girl, formidable casino tycoon Marcus Carrera swooped in to the rescue. Their mutual attraction sizzled from the start, but could this tempestuous duo survive the forces conspiring against them?

#1646 THE MARRIAGE ACT—Elissa Ambrose
The Parks Empire

Red-haired beauty Linda Mailer didn't want her unexpected pregnancy to tempt Tyler Dalton into a pity proposal. But the green-eyed cop convinced Linda that, at least for the child's sake, a temporary marriage was in order. Their loveless marriage was headed for wedded bliss when business suddenly got in the way of their pleasure....

#1647 THE SHEIK & THE PRINCESS BRIDE—
Susan Mallery
Desert Rogues

From the moment they met, flight instructor Billie Van Horn's sexy good looks and charming personality blew Prince Jefri away. Their mutual love burned hot, but when Jefri was suddenly presented with an arranged marriage, he found himself unable to love the woman he had—or have the woman he loved. Could Jefri successfully trade tradition for true love?

#1648 A BABY ON THE RANCH—Stella Bagwell
Men of the West

When Lonnie Corteen agreed to search for his best friend's long-lost sister, he found the beautiful Katherine McBride pregnant, alone and in no mood to have her heart trampled on again. But Lonnie wanted to reunite her family—and become a part of it.

#1649 WANTED: ONE FATHER—Penny Richards

Single dad Max Murdock needed a quiet place to write and a baby-sitter for his daughter. Zoe Barlow had a cabin to rent and needed some extra cash. What began as a perfect match blossomed into the perfect romance. But could this lead to one big perfect family?

#1650 THE WAY TO A WOMAN'S HEART—Carol A. Voss

Nan Kramer had lost one man in the line of fire and wasn't about to put herself and her three children through losing another. Family friend—and local deputy—David Elliot agreed that because of his high-risk job, he should remain unattached. Nonetheless, David had found his way into this woman's heart, and neither wanted to send him packing....